The Motion Demon

THE MOTION DEMON

Stefan Grabinski

Translated by
Miroslaw Lipinski

NoHo Press
New York City

The Motion Demon
Stefan Grabinski

Cover illustration based on Margit Schwarcz Lithograph, 1931

First Polish edition published in 1919.
Ash-Tree Press hardcover edition published in 2005
NoHo Press paperbound edition January 2014
Translation and Introduction © Miroslaw Lipinski 2005
New material © Miroslaw Lipinski 2014

CONTENTS

Introduction 7
Engine Driver Grot... 13
The Wandering Train 28
The Motion Demon 36
The Sloven 49
The Perpetual Passenger 60
In the Compartment 71
Signals 83
The Siding 93
Ultima Thule... 116

INTRODUCTION

One of the most important voices in fantastique literature, Stefan Grabinski, was born in the small town of Kamionka Strumilowa, Poland on February 26, 1887. Not part of any literary clique or movement, he suffered for his originality and the limitations imposed on him by being a writer in a country that did not fully recognize his work or take it seriously. Sickly and suffering from bone tuberculosis at an early age, Grabinski became seduced by the supernatural and introverted explorations into the mysteries of life. For his daily bread, he worked as a teacher in a secondary school, but his passion was writing strange fictions that focused on his atypical concerns and interests.

In "O tworczosci fantastycznej" (*Lwowskie Wiadomosci Muzyczne i Literackie*, no. 10, 1928), Stefan Grabinski proposed calling his fiction work "psychofantasy" or "metafantasy." Unlike straightforward, conventional fantasy that displayed the outward and ornamental, this type of fantasy would source psychological, philosophical, or metaphysical concerns. Most of Grabinski's fiction shares this inner-investigatory drive, with added impulses. "Wonder and fear—these are my guiding motives," Grabinski wrote in "Wyznania" (*Polonia*, no.141, 1926). Also unmistakable in his work is a keen sense of individualism, even an unapologetic misanthropy, and a resultant predilection to choose as his protagonists solitary men who travel along little explored paths and are proud of doing so. An opponent of mechanism, Grabinski alerted the modern world to forces supernatural and unexpected that would never go away, no matter how materially advanced and spiritually disregardful the world would become. For Grabinski, one of the most puzzling forces, equally dangerous and liberating, was the human mind itself, and the Polish writer became a master at tracing neurotic constructs, insane theorems, and hyper phobias. Yet whatever the madness, Grabinski loved his lunatics, for they shared with him a maverick quality that was born of the spirit and of an individualistic, albeit at times wayward, intellect.

A short self-published volume of stories, *Z wyjaktow. W pomrokach wiary (From the Unusual. In the Shadows of Belief,* 1909), under the pseudonym Stefan Zalny, went unnoticed, but Grabinski's official debut, *Na wgorzu roz* (*On the Hill of Roses,* 1918), caught the attention of a renowned Polish critic, Karol Irzykowski, who wrote: "Rarely in our country does an artistic debut exhibit so distinct an individuality." ("Fantastyka," *Maski,* no. 33, 1918.) The six-story collection showcased splendidly Grabinski's unique themes centered on aberrant psychology and the supernatural forces that lie in wait for vengeance or malicious notice. Indeed, nothing like this had appeared in Polish literature before—nor in supernatural fiction worldwide had anyone bothered with the analysis.

With rail travel being the dominant mode of quick transportation at the time, it was Grabinski's next short story collection, *Demon ruchu* (*The Motion Demon,* 1919), which made the most impact in Poland, though the book's influence could not extend farther due to a lack of Polish translators and an international lack of healthy interest in Polish literature. Compiling the train stories that he had written for magazines and newspapers, Grabinski used the train world as a metaphor for life's energies and impulses, as he merged the "vital energy" theories of Henri Bergson with the theories of motion promoted by scientists like Newton and Einstein. Memorable mavericks people these stories, where even a simple thing such as a train ride can offer telling clues to the metaphysical and the beyond. The book was popular enough to warrant a second, expanded edition in 1922. In the years before his death, Grabinski had hopes for a third edition, with more added stories, but his dream was not realized.

Grabinski's next collection, *Szalony patnik* (*The Insane Pilgrim*, 1920), further explored the wayward consciousness and included Grabinski's supreme artistic statement, "The Area." In the story, Grabinski's alter-ego, Wrzesmian, secludes himself in a lonely house at the outskirts of town. His eyes and spirit fixated on a deserted mansion opposite him, he dreams to life peculiar people who inhabit the building, and who, one night, compel him to step outside the safety of his abode and fully enter into a dream world of his creations—with tragic results. The activation of thought, its source as the seed of reality, is key to understanding the power Grabinski gave to ideas and the supernatural. Unlike many a fantasist, he believed in the supernatural meanings of what he wrote. None of his works were simple entertainments; they all carried the power of an idea and the impression of a sincere, yearning soul.

Ksiega ognia (*The Book of Fire*, 1922) returned Grabinski to a collection centered on a single subject matter—fire this time. Reading these stories, so artfully constructed, it is impossible not to be affected by them and consider the fire element from a primal, respectful, and fearing perspective, which was, in part, Grabinski's intent.

In the 1920s Grabinski sought newer creative horizons in longer formats, and his short story output began to decrease considerably after the publication of *Niesamowita opowiesc* (*An Uncanny Tale*, 1922), which continued Grabinski's precise and perceptive journeys into the mind and the supernatural. His first novel, *Salamandra* (*The Salamander*), written in the fall and winter of 1922, but appearing in print two years later, in 1924, contains a flavourfully bold description of the Sabbath, yet modern tastes may have difficulty with the book's heavy dependency on the occult and its terminology.

Cien Bafometa (*Baphomet's Shadow*, 1926) is probably Grabinski's most fully realized and successful longer work. It deals with the traditional subject of Good vs. Evil, but introduces an original compendium of sinister, seemingly disjointed events to comment powerfully on moral responsibility. Pawelek Kuternozka, the devilish seller of religious objects, takes his place as one of the most memorable characters in supernatural fiction, and Wrzesmian, the master fantasist of "The Area," turns up in a chapter to render service to his creator by countering superficial critics, who were already attacking Grabinski's work with snobbish glee. Grabinski's subsequent novels, *Klasztor i morze* (*The Cloister and the Sea*, 1928) and *Wyspa Itongo* (*Itongo Island*, 1936), failed to make an impression on the book market, though they contained unique concepts and highly original passages. His final short story collection, *Namietnosc* (*Passion*, 1930), was maturely full-bodied, but likewise failed to make a mark.

Grabinski's fragile health began seriously to affect his output in these later years. He died of complications from tuberculosis on November 12, 1936, in poverty and neglected by society and the literary establishment. Before he died, he complained bitterly about having been misunderstood and forgotten in his native land. Yet vindication would come.

Interest in "the Polish Poe" began to rise in Poland in the late 1950s and increase in the 1960s and 1970s, with reprints of many of his stories, including a collection edited by the Polish science-fiction master, Stanislaw Lem. Several films based on his work were produced for Polish television, and a feature film, based on Grabinski's early short story "At the Villa by the Sea," was exhibited in theatres. West Germany picked up on the fascination with German translations. In the United States, my home-manufactured journal, *The Grabinski Reader* (1986–90), heralded the first translations of Grabinski's work in English and became favorably noticed by such writers as Robert Bloch, Colin Wilson, and a then-young Thomas Ligotti. These translations, and other stories translated by me for horror fiction magazines, were collected in *The Dark Domain* (Dedalus/Hippocrene), published in England at the end of 1993. This book garnered welcome attention, with respected weird fiction author China Mieville becoming a champion of Grabinski's work.

Grabinski's influence increased when young film-makers outside Poland began adopting the author's stories for noteworthy short films. One such film-maker, Holger Mandel, even held a Stefan Grabinski evening at the Museum of Literature at Oberrhein, Germany on June 12, 2004. His two Grabinski short films were exhibited, and readings and a musical performance were held. Surely, this was the first such literary event in Grabinskiana.

As the new millennium progressed, Poland began to awaken more and more to Grabinski's worth and standing as one of the great writers of supernatural fiction. 2012 became "The Year of Grabinski," with symposia and scholarly works dedicated to the writer appearing with commendable frequency.

The growing, steady recognition of Stefan Grabinski means that the future looks bright for an author who was once dismissed in his own country and then forgotten, and whose work was, at one point, completely unknown outside Poland. As with the creations who blossomed to life from pure thought in Grabinski's "The Area," the stories of Grabinski, emerging from his imagination nearly a century ago, are ready to live again and impress with their wonderments and instruct with their thrilling, tenacious suggestions.

Miroslaw Lipinski
August 2005
Updated November 2013

ENGINE DRIVER GROT

From the railway station at Brzan came the following dispatch to the stationmaster of Podwyz: "Be on the alert for express number ten! The engine driver is either drunk or insane."

The stationmaster, a tall, bony blond with sandy sideburns, read the roll once, twice; he cut off the thin white ribbon that had spun out from the block and, coiling it in a ring around his finger, slipped it into his pocket. A quick glance thrown at the station clock informed him that there was still enough time for the train in question. So he yawned in boredom, nonchalantly lit up a cigarette, and went over to the adjoining room of the cashier, the fair-haired, squat Miss Feli, a casual ideal in moments of boredom and in anticipation of a better morsel.

While the stationmaster was so suitably preparing himself for the reception of the announced locomotive, the suspect train had already travelled a considerable distance beyond the Brzan station.

The hour was most wonderful. The hot June sun had past its zenith and was sowing golden rays throughout the earth. Villages and hamlets with flowery apple and cherry trees flashed by, meadows and haystacks were flung backward in green sheets. The train sped along at full steam: here it was snatched up by the arms of rustling pine and spruce forests, there, emerging from the embrace of trees, it was greeted by bowing grain fields. Far in the horizon, a misty blue line indicated a range of mountains. . . .

Leaning against the flank of the engine, Grot set a steady glance through the little oval window at the space unreeling in a lengthy, grey course framed by the dark rails. The train crept along these rails lightly, predatorily, straddling them with an iron system of wheels and eagerly sweeping them underneath.

The engine driver felt an almost physical pleasure from this continual conquest, which, never satiated, lets go of the already fallen prey with disregard and speeds on to new conquests. Grot loved to vanquish space!

Looking intently at the line of track, he would frequently become thoughtful, contemplative, forgetful of the world, until his stoker had to tug at his arm and give notice that the pressure was too great for the station already close at hand. Yet Grot was a first-class engine driver.

He loved his occupation above all and would not have changed it for anything in the world. He had entered railway service relatively late, when he was thirty, but, despite this, he immediately displayed such a sure hand at running a locomotive that he quickly surpassed his more experienced comrades.

What he had been before, no one knew. When questioned, he would reluctantly answer this and that, or else remain stubbornly silent.

His colleagues and the railway authorities held him in evident respect, singling him out from others. In his brief words, parsimoniously distributed among people, he revealed an uncommon intelligence, a compelling sense of honor.

There were various, frequently contradictory rumors afloat about him and his past. Yet everyone held the unanimous opinion that Christopher Grot was a so-called stray individual, something of a fallen star, one of those who should have gone along a higher path, but, thanks to the fatalism of life, became stranded on the rocks.

He seemed unaware of this situation, however, and did not feel sorry for himself. He performed his duties willingly and never asked for vacations. Whether he had forgotten about what had once occurred, whether he did not feel called upon to attain higher aims—no one knew.

Two facts had been established from Grot's past: the first, that he had served in the army during the Franco-Prussian campaign; the second, that he had lost his beloved brother at that time.

Despite all sorts of endeavors by the curious, no one was able to draw out any further details. Finally, people simply gave up, content with the meagre biographical bouquet of "Engineer Grot." So they eventually called, for no specific reason, their taciturn fellow railwayman. This nickname—given him, incidentally, without any malicious intent—somehow blended so well with the person of the engine driver that even the authorities tolerated it in orders and decrees. In this manner people made note of his distinct character.

The machine worked hard, breathing out every moment puffs of fluffy, ruffled smoke. The steam, constantly fanned by the zealous hand of the stoker, was overflowing the blowpipes along the skeleton of the iron colossus, pushing valves, struggling with pistons, driving wheels. Rails rattled, gears creaked, frantic cranks and plates roared. . . .

Momentarily, Grot woke up from his reveries and glanced at the pressure gauge. The needle, marking the arch, was nearing the fatal number thirteen.

"Release steam!"

The stoker stretched out his hand and pulled on the valve; a prolonged, piercing whistle resounded, while at the same time a tiny milk-white funnel bloomed from the side of the machine.

Grot folded his arms across his chest and once again sank into reveries.

"'Engineer Grot' — ha, ha! A most accurate nickname! People don't even suspect how accurate!"

Suddenly, the engine driver saw in the distant, hazy vista of years gone-by a quiet, modest little house in a suburb of the capital. In the bright centre room stands a large table covered with piles of diagrams, strange drawings, technical sketches. Leaning over one of these is the flaxen head of Olek, his younger brother. Beside him stands he, Christopher, running his finger along a sapphire line circling elliptically over some mathematical plane. Olek nods, corrects something, explains....

This is their workshop—this is their secret interior from which was hatched the bold idea of an airplane that, flying freely about space, would have conquered the atmosphere and broadened man's mind, lifting it to the beyond, to infinity. Not much more time was needed to finish off the work: a month, two months—three, at most. All of a sudden the war came, then recruitment, the march, a battle, and ... death. Olek's bright-haired head dropped to his blood-stained chest, his blue eyes closed forever....

Grot remembered that one moment, that horrible moment of scaling to the top of the enemy fort. Olek had dashed forward heroically and was seen from a distance at the front of the detachment. His drawn sabre was shaving with its blade cuttings of colorful proportion, his manly hand was seizing his flag-staff in a victorious grasp. Suddenly a flash came from the ramparts, a swirl of smoke jetted from the fort's stronghold, a hellish explosion rocked the battlements. Olek reeled, wavered under the glimmering rainbow of the released sword, and tumbled down—on the threshold of battle plans, at the very moment of soldierly realizations, at the moment of reaching the goal....

His death affected Christopher badly. For many months Christopher Grot was laid up with malignant fever in a field hospital. Afterwards, he returned to civilian life a broken man. He abandoned his old ideas, his revolutionary concepts, his plans of conquest: he became an engine driver. He sensed the compromise, he understood the travesty, but he had no more strength left; he was content to deal in miniature. Soon the substitute ideal completely replaced the original one, covering with its narrow, dull framework the previously wide horizon: he now conquered space on a new, smaller scale. But he had entreated the railway authorities for only express rides—he never drove ordinary trains. In this manner, gaining in this terrain, he at least came closer to the original concept. He was intoxicated with a wild ride on far-spanning lines, dazed by the conquest of considerable distances within a short period of time.

But he could not stand return journeys; he detested the so-called *tour-retour* trips. Grot only liked speeding on to what was ahead of him—he loathed any repetitions. That is why he preferred to return to the inevitable point of departure by roundabout routes, by a line circular or elliptical, anything but the same one. He understood perfectly the deficiency of curves that revert back to themselves, he felt the unethicalness of these continually inbred roads, but was saved by the appearance of progressive motion; he had the illusion, at least, that he was going forward.

For Grot's ideal was a frenzied ride in a straight line, without deviations, without circulations, a breathless, insane ride without stops, the whirling rush of the engine into the distant bluish mist, a winged run into infinity.

Grot could not bear any type of goal. Since the time of his brother's tragic death a particular psychic complex had developed within him: dread before any aim, before any type of end, any limits. With all his might he fell in love with the perpetuality of constantly going forward, the toil of reaching ahead. He detested the realization of goals; he trembled before the moment of their fulfilment in fear that, in that last crucial moment, a disappointment would overtake him, a cord would break, that he would tumble down into the abyss—as had Olek years ago.

Because of this, the engine driver felt a natural dread of stations and pauses. Admittedly, he had few of them along his way, but they were always there, and one had to stop the train from time to time.

Eventually a station became for him a symbol of a detested end, a formative materialization of planned goals, that cursed aim before which he was seized with repugnance and fear.

The ideal line of track was broken down into a series of segments, each segment a closed unit from the point of departure to the point of arrival. A disappointing limitation arose, tight, banal in the fullest sense of the word: here—there. On the taut, wonderful projection into boundlessness there were dull junctions and stubborn kinks that spoiled momentum, tainted fury.

For the time being he saw no help anywhere: from the nature of things a train had to halt once in a while at some loathsome stop.

And when the contours of a station's buildings appeared on the horizon, he fell into an indescribable dread and disgust; the hand raised over the crank would draw back involuntarily, and he would have to use the entire strength of his will not to pass the station.

Finally, when his inner opposition grew to an unprecedented pitch, he came upon a happy idea: he decided to introduce a certain freedom to the range of the goal by moving its boundary points. Thanks to this, the concept of a station, losing a lot of its exactness, became something general, something lightly sketched and most elastic. This shifting of the boundaries granted a certain freedom of movement, it did not completely muzzle the brake. The stopping points, acquiring the character of fluidity, transformed the name of the station into a vague, cavalier, almost fictional term with which one did not have to reckon as much; in a word, a station given such a wide understanding, submitting to the engine driver's interpretation, was now less threatening, though still abhorrent.

It therefore became a question, above all, of never stopping the train at the place marked by regulations, but always to lean out beyond or before it.

Grot initially proceeded with utmost caution, so as not to awaken the suspicions of officials; the deviations were at first so slight that no one paid any attention. Wanting, however, to strengthen within himself a feeling of freedom, the engine driver introduced a certain diversity: one time he would stop too early, the other time too late—these shifts vacillated from one side to the other.

But eventually this caution began to irritate him; his freedom seemed a sham, an illusion, something in the manner of a self-deception; the calm spread over the faces of stationmasters, not befuddled by surprise, annoyed him, awakening the spirit of contrariness and rebellion. Grot became audacious. The variations became stronger with each day; the range grew and intensified.

Already yesterday the stationmaster at Smaglowa, a grizzly fellow with constant half-open eyes like an old fox, had been squinting suspiciously at the train that had stopped a good distance from the station. Grot even thought that the stationmaster had muttered something, while motioning in his direction. But somehow he got away scot free.

The engine driver had rubbed his hands and rejoiced: "They've noticed!"

Leaving Wrotycz at daybreak, he decided to double the stakes.

"I wonder in what proportion will these gentlemen's irritation rise?" he thought, releasing the spigot into motion. "I would suppose to the nth degree."

Somehow his conjecture did not fall short of expectation. This day's entire trip would be one uninterrupted series of disturbances.

It began in Zaszum, the first major stop on the line, which he had intended to pass. Smiling maliciously under his moustache, he stopped the train a kilometer before the station. Leaning against the engine's sill, Grot lit his pipe, and, puffing on it leisurely, he observed with interest the amazed faces of the conductors and the chief supervisor, who could not explain the behavior of the engine driver. Several passengers tilted out their startled heads and glanced to the right and to the left, undoubtedly thinking some obstacle had hindered the train's movement. Finally the stationmaster ran up and asked what was happening.

"Why didn't you come up to the platform? No obstruction was signalled; everything is in order."

Grot slowly let out a large, dense puff of smoke, and not removing the pipe from his lips, he eased out coolly through his teeth:

"Hmm . . . is that so? It seemed to me that the switch was badly set. It doesn't pay to drive up this short distance: my old lady is a little out of breath." He tenderly tapped the barrel of the furnace. "Besides, the passengers are getting off by themselves—see for yourself—ah, there's one, two; there goes an entire family."

Indeed. Tired of waiting, the passengers were beginning to abandon the cars, and stooping from the weight of bundles and luggage, they were making their way to the station. With an ironical glance Grot followed their movement, not giving a thought to changing his tactic.

The stationmaster frowned slightly and, giving up on the situation, reprimanded Grot upon parting.

"In the future try straining your eyes better!"

The engine driver dismissed the rebuke with contemptuous silence. A couple of minutes later, ignoring the station, the train was gliding along on its journey.

At Brzan, the next station stop, almost the identical story repeated itself, the only difference being that this time Grot fancied stopping the train a kilometer beyond the station. Here he did as he pleased and did not go back to the platform. He noticed, however, before he moved on, the supervisor of the train whispering something intently to the stationmaster. Grot realized from their glances and gestures that he was the subject of the conversation, but pretended not to notice. He was amused, though, by the characteristic "he's crazy" circle drawn on the forehead by the finger of the red-capped official. Shortly thereafter, he was speeding along at full steam, unaware that the telegraph in Brzan was warning the station authorities at Podwyz.

And he was not far from that city. The late-afternoon sky was already lined by the golden crosses of churches, coils of smoke were passing over a sea of roofs, factory spires were cracking sharply. Already one could see in the distance the track system intersecting, a forest of switches darkening the area, the distance marker.

Grot grasped the crank vigorously, set the lever, turned the brake; the engine let out a plaintive complaint, part moan, part whistle; it spit out through its ribs a mighty waterfall of steam and settled down in place: the train stood a good one and a half kilometers before the station.

Grot withdrew his hand from the taps and studied the effect. He did not have to wait long. The already-biased stationmaster sent out a junior-ranking comrade in the role of a parliamentarian.

The young man had a stern, almost compressed expression. He straightened himself up, stiffly pulled on his service jacket, and ceremoniously ascended to the engine platform.

"Drive up to the station!"

Grot silently grasped the crank, set the pistons in motion: the train moved.

The assistant, proud of his triumphant accomplishment, crossed his arms Napoleonically and, turning scornfully away from the engine driver, he lit a cigarette.

But his success was illusory. For the train, ignoring the platform, roared on, and instead of stopping at the station, it travelled a considerable distance beyond it, only to halt there for a rest, puffing out all its steam.

At first the official was unaware of what had occurred; only when he noticed the station building behind his left side did he advance threateningly towards the engine driver.

"Have you gone crazy? Stopping a train in an open field! Either you're mad or you've been drinking too much today! Go back instantly!"

Grot did not budge, he did not move from his place. The official shoved him roughly away from the furnace, and taking his post, he let go of the counter steam; after a moment the train drew back puffingly to the platform.

Grot did not interfere. Some particular apathy overpowered his movements, fettered his hands. He looked blankly at the faces of the rail service, functionaries and clerks who had flocked around his engine; he passively allowed himself to be pulled down from the platform—like an automaton he followed a summoning official.

After a couple of minutes he found himself in the station office, in front of a large, green wool-covered table where apparatuses were incessantly snapping in nervous jolts, long ribbons were spinning out from blocks, little bells were fluttering.

The stationmaster would interrogate him. The clerk sitting by his side dipped his pen in ink and waited anxiously for the questions that would fall from his supervisor's lips.

Somehow they fell.

"Name?"

"Christopher Grot."

"Age?"

"Thirty-two."

"At what time did you depart Wrotycz?"

"This morning at 4:54."

"Did you inspect the engine before taking over the train?"

"I inspected it."

"Do you remember its serial and number?"

A strange smile flashed across Grot's face:

"I remember. Serial: zero; number: infinity."

The stationmaster glanced knowingly at his transcribing colleague.

"Please write down the numbers you've just given me on this piece of paper."

The stationmaster slipped him a sheet of paper and a pencil.

Grot shrugged his shoulders.

"Certainly."

And he drew two separate signs:

0 ∞

The stationmaster glanced at the numbers, shook his head, and continued with the questioning:

"The number of the trailer?"

"I don't remember."

"That's bad, very bad—an engine driver should know such things," he opined sententiously.

"What is your stoker's name?" he asked after a brief pause.

"Blazej Midget."

"The forename is correct, but the surname is wrong."

"I've spoken the truth."

"You're mistaken; his name is Blazej Sad."

Grot waved his hand indifferently.

"That could be. To me, his name is Midget."

Once again the stationmaster exchanged a meaningful glance with his companion.

"The conductor's name?"

"Stanislaw Ant."

The examiner held back with difficulty an outburst of laughter.

"Ant, you say? Ant? Ah, that's good one! That's fabulous—Ant?!"

"Yes. Stanislaw Ant."

"No, Mr Grot. The name of the conductor of your train is Stanislaw Zywiecki. Again you are mistaken."

The recording clerk leaned his pomaded head towards his chief and whispered in his ear.

"Stationmaster, this person is either drunk or a bit touched in the head."

"It seems the latter," answered the official, clearing his throat; after which, he turned back to the culprit with a new question.

"Are you married?"

"No."

"Did you have anything to drink before your departure?"

"I detest alcohol."

"How many hours have you been at work?"

"Sixteen."

"You don't feel tired?"

"Not at all."

"Why did you not stop your train four consecutive times at the designated place before a station?"

Grot was silent. He could not, he did not want to reveal this for anything in the world.

"I'm waiting for an answer."

The engine driver hung his head in gloom.

The stationmaster raised himself solemnly from the desk and pronounced judgment.

"Now you'll go and get some sleep. A colleague will replace you. I'm suspending you for the time being; it's possible that you'll be asked back sometime in the future. Meanwhile, I would advise you to seek a doctor's care as soon as possible. You're seriously ill."

Grot turned white, he staggered. The affair took on a tragic character. From the stationmaster's facial expression, the tone and content of his words, he realized that he was considered a madman. He understood that he had lost his position, that he had stopped being an engine driver.

"Stationmaster, I am completely healthy," he moaned out, wringing his hands. "I can drive on."

'That's out of the question, Mr Grot. I cannot entrust the fate of several hundred people to you. Do you know that you almost were the cause of a collision today? You rode up too far, reaching a point where a crossing would have occurred with the Czerniaw passenger train. If your assistant hadn't moved back your train, a collision would surely have resulted. The already signalled-forward train arrived two minutes late. You are not fit for duty, Mr Grot. You first have to undergo treatment. Besides, we are finished. Please leave the premises."

With a heavy, leaden step Grot exited the room; he tramped the platform, halting and reeling like a drunkard, and dragged himself along railway warehouses.

His skull was bursting with a dull pain, his heart sobbed despair. He had lost his post.

It did not matter about the paltry several dozen pieces of coin, a job or a position—what mattered was the engine, without which he did not know how to live. It concerned the invaluable, solely available means with which he could grapple with space, with which he could speed to obscure distances. With the loss of his post the ground was removed from under him, and the black, fathomless abyss of a purposeless life opened up.

Attacked by a choking pain in his larynx, he passed the warehouses; he passed the bridge, the tunnel, and mechanically went onto the tracks.

He was already far from the station. Stumbling at every step against the timbered groundwork that crossed the rails, bumping into switches, Grot wandered among the coldly glittering iron.

Suddenly he heard behind him a heavy groan, he felt the trembling of the earth under his feet. He turned around and slowly became aware of a gliding, detached engine.

He took it in with the eye of an expert, ascertained the abundance of coal in the trailer, and joyfully noticed the absence of the stoker.

A decision as quick as a flash, as a flicker of an eyelid, throbbed in his troubled brain and ripened immediately.

With a careful, predatory step, a stalking step like a panther's, he went to the side of the iron monster and in one spring jumped to the platform.

The movement was so sudden and unexpected that it stupefied the driver of the engine. Before the driver could orient himself to the situation created by his new guest, Grot gagged his mouth with a kerchief, fettered his hands crosswise, and, laying him on the engine's floor, pushed him from the running-board towards the earth.

Dealing with this in the course of several minutes, Grot then took over his predecessor's place by the furnace.

A titanic joy was bursting in his heart—a cry of triumph erupted from his chest. He was once again at the controls!

He pressed the spigots, tugged on the steam, turned the whining crank. The engine, as if sensing the hand of a master, quivered at being employed; it coughed with a robust, parting whistle, and moved forth into the wide world. Grot went insane from intoxication. Emerging from the labyrinth of rails, he entered the main track that sped along straight ahead like an arrow and swooped forward into space!

A gale-like speed commenced, unhampered by anything, uninterrupted by stops or monotonous halts. Grot passed indistinct stations like lightning, he flashed by indistinct towns like a demon, flew through indistinct halting places like a hurricane. Without pause he scooped coals with a shovel, threw them into the furnace; he fed the fire, compressed the steam. Like a man possessed, he ran from trailer to furnace, from furnace to trailer; he checked the water level on the meter, he inspected the steam pressure.

He saw nothing, he thought nothing—he only drank in speed, he only lived for rushing motion, he plunged himself into the gigantism of momentum. He lost count of time, what part of day it was, what hour. He did not know how long the hellish ride had lasted so far—a day, two days, or a week....

The engine ran riot. The wheels, frenzied with speed, carried out unattainable, fantastically swift revolutions; the overstrained pistons retracted, then eagerly pushed forward again; the possessed, breathless copper bins rattled. The needle on the pressure gauge went continually up—the red-hot furnace belched out fire, scorched the skin, burned the palms. That's nothing! More! Further on! Faster! Full speed ahead! Full speed ahead!

A new heap of coal vanished into the abyss of the furnace and spattered a bunch of blood-like sparks—a new jet of steam shot blazing heat into melting pipes....

Grot fixed his feverish eyes on the ruby mouth of the furnace and drank in its swelter, sucked in its blood. . . .

Suddenly—something surged, something hooted with a devilish whine—an explosion resounded, as if from a thousand cannons, thunder roared, as if from a hundred lightning bolts. A fiery, entangled cloud burst forth, a confused column of fragments, iron hulls, bent sheet metal. Under the sky sputtered a rocket of bits and pieces, ripped-apart spans, blown-up bells. . . .

The pall of night was rent asunder by Grot's crimson end.

THE WANDERING TRAIN

Feverish activity reigned at the Horsk train station. It was right before the holidays, an eagerly anticipated time when people could take off from work for a few days. The platform swarmed with those arriving and departing. Women's excited faces flashed by, colorful hat ribbons flapped around, frantic rushing marked every scene. Here, the slender cylinder of an elegant gentleman's top hat pushed through the crowds; there, a priest's black cassock could be seen; elsewhere, under arcades, soldiers in blue squeezed through the crush; nearby, workers in their grey shirts tried to make their way in the press. Exuberant life seethed, and strained against the confines of the station, it overflowed noisily beyond its area. The chaotic bustle of the passengers, the exhortations of the porters, the sound of whistles, the noise of released steam all merged into a giddy symphony in which one became lost, surrendering the diminished, deafened self onto the waves of a mighty element to be carried, rocked, dazed. . . .

The railway employees were working at an intense pace. Traffic officials, conspicuous in their red caps, appeared everywhere—giving orders, clearing the absent-minded from the tracks, and passing a swift, vigilant eye on the trains at their moment of departure. Conductors were in a constant rush, walking with speedy steps through the lengthy coaches. Master signalmen, the pilots of the station, executed concise and efficient instructions—commands for departure. Everything went along at a brisk tempo, marked off to the minute, to the second—everyone's eyes were involuntarily checking the time on the white double-dial clock above.

Yet a quiet spectator standing to the side would, after a brief observation, have received impressions incompatible with the ostensible order of things.

Something had slipped into the standard regulations and traditional course of activities; some type of undefined, though weighty, obstacle opposed the sacred smoothness of rail travel.

One could tell this from the nervous, exaggerated gestures of the railwaymen and their restless glances and anticipating faces. Something had broken down in the previously exemplary system. Some unhealthy, terrible current circulated along its hundredfold-branched arteries, and it permeated the surface in half-conscious flashes.

The zeal of the railwaymen reflected their obvious willingness to overcome whatever had stealthily wormed its way into a perfect structure. Everyone was in two or three places at once to suppress forcefully this irritating nightmare, to subordinate it to the regular demands of work, to the wearisome but safe equilibrium of routine chores.

This was, after all, their area, their "region," exercised through many years of diligent application, a terrain, it seemed, that they knew through and through. They were, after all, exponents of that work ethic, that sphere of practical activity, where to them, the initiated, nothing should be unclear, where they, the representatives and sole interpreters of the entire complicated train system, could not, and should not, be caught unawares by any type of enigma. Why, for a long time everything had been calculated, weighed, measured—everything, though complex, had not passed human understanding—and everywhere there was a precise moderation without surprises, a regularity of repeated occurrences foreseen from the start!

They felt, then, a collective responsibility towards the dense mass of the travelling public to whom was owed complete peace and safety.

Meanwhile their inner perplexity, flowing in vexatious waves over the passengers, was sensed by the public.

If the problem had concerned a so-called "accident," which, admittedly, one could not foresee but for which an explanation could be provided afterwards, then they, the professionals, were vulnerable but certainly not desperate. But something totally different was at issue here.

Something incalculable like a chimera, capricious like madness had arrived, and it shattered with one blow the traditional arrangement of things.

Therefore, they were ashamed of themselves and humiliated before the public.

At present it was most important that the problem should not spread, that "the general public" should not find out anything about it. It was appropriate to conceal any counter-measures, so that this strange affair would not come to light in the newspapers and create a public uproar.

Thus far the matter had been miraculously confined to the circle of railwaymen connected with it. A truly amazing solidarity united these people: they were silent. They communicated with each other by telling glances, specific gestures, and a play on well-chosen words. Thus far the public did not know anything about any problem.

Yet the restlessness of the railway employees and the nervousness of the officials had been gradually transmitted, creating a receptive soil for the sowing of secret conspiracies.

And "the problem" was indeed strange and puzzling.

For a certain time there had appeared on the nation's railways a train not included in any generally known register, not entered in the count of circulating locomotives—in a word, an intruder without patent or sanction. One could not even state what category it belonged to or from what factory it had originated, as the momentary brief length of time it allowed itself to be seen made any determination in this respect impossible. In any event, judging by the incredible speed with which it moved before the dumbfounded eyes of onlookers, it had to occupy a very high standing among trains: at the very least it was an express.

Yet most distressing was its unpredictability. The intruder turned up everywhere, suddenly appearing from some railway line to fly by with a devilish roar along the tracks before disappearing in the distance. One day it had been seen near the station at M.; the following day it appeared in an open field beyond the town of W.; a couple of days later it flew by with petrifying impudence near a lineman's booth in the district of G.

At first it was thought that the insane train belonged to an existing line and that only tardiness, or a mistake by the officials concerned, had failed to ascertain its identity. Therefore, inquiries began, endless signalling and communications between stations—all to no avail: the intruder simply sneered at the endeavors of the officials, usually appearing where it was least expected.

Particularly disheartening was the circumstance that nowhere could one catch, overtake, or stop it. Several planned pursuits to this end on one of the most technologically advanced engines created a horrible fiasco: the terrible train immediately took the lead.

Then the railway personnel began to be seized by a superstitious fear and a stifled rage. An unheard of thing! For quite a few years the coaches and cars had run according to an established plan that had been worked out at headquarters and approved by government officials—for years everything had been calculated, more or less foreseen, and when some "mistake" or "oversight" occurred, it could be logically explained and corrected. Then suddenly an uninvited guest slips onto the tracks, spoiling the order of things, turning regulations upside down, and bringing confusion and disarray to a well-regulated organization!

Thank goodness the interloper had not brought about any disaster. This was something that generally puzzled them from the very beginning. The train always appeared on a track that was free at the time; so far the crazy train had not caused a collision. Yet one could occur any day. Indeed, that was where things seemed to be heading. With mounting dread, a tendency in its movements was discovered which indicated that the train was entering into closer contact with its normal comrades. Though initially it seemed to steer clear of such close contact, appearing considerable distances beyond or before other trains, these days it sprang up at the backs of its predecessors after the passage of ever-shorter intervals of time. Already it had shot by an express on its way to O.; a week ago it barely avoided a passenger train between S. and F.; the other day only by a miracle did it not crash into the express from W.

Stationmasters trembled at the news of these near misses. Only double tracks and the quick judgment of engine drivers had prevented a collision. These amazing escapes had recently begun to occur with more frequency, so that the chances of a happy way out of a collision seemed to diminish daily.

From its role as the hunted, the intruder went into an active, magnetic-like impulse towards what was running smoothly and generally understood. The insane train began directly to menace the old order of things. The affair could end tragically any day now.

For a month the stationmaster at Horsk had been leading an unpleasant existence. In constant anxiety over an unexpected visit of the mysterious train, he was almost continually vigilant, not deserting day or night the signal-box that had been entrusted to him nearly a year ago as a token of recognition for "his energy and uncommon efficiency." And the post was important, for at the Horsk station several principal railway lines intersected and the traffic of the entire country was concentrated.

Today, faced with a greatly increased number of passengers, his work was particularly difficult.

Evening was slowly falling. Electric lights flashed up, reflectors threw off their powerful projections. By the green fires of the junction-signals, rails started to glitter with a gloomy metallic glaze that curved along with the cold iron serpents. Here and there, in the shadowy twilight, a conductor's lamp flickered faintly, a lineman's signal blinked. In the distance, far beyond the station, where the emerald eyes of lanterns were being extinguished, a semaphore was making night signals.

Here, leaving its horizontal position, the arm of the semaphore rose to an angle of forty-five degrees: the passenger train from Brzesk was approaching.

One could already hear the panting respiration of the locomotive, the rhythmic clatter of the wheels; one could already see the bright-yellow glass at its front. The train is heading into the station. . . .

From its open windows lean out the golden locks of children, the curious faces of women; welcoming kerchiefs are waved.

The throngs waiting on the platform push violently towards the coaches, outstretched hands on both sides tend towards a meeting. . . .

What kind of commotion is that to the right? Strident whistles rend the air. The stationmaster is shouting something in a hoarse, wild voice.

"Away! Get back, run! Reverse steam! Backwards! Backwards! . . . Collision!"

The masses throw themselves in a dense onrush towards the banisters, breaking them. Frenzied eyes instinctively look to the right—where the railway employees have gathered—and see the spasmodic, aimlessly frantic vibrations of lanterns endeavoring to turn back a train, which, with its entire momentum, is coming from the opposite side of the track occupied by the Brzesk passenger train. Shrill whistles cut the desperate responses of bugles and the hellish tumult of people. In vain! The unexpected locomotive is getting closer, with terrifying velocity; the enormous green lights of the engine weirdly push aside the darkness, the powerful pistons move with fabulous, possessed efficiency.

From a thousand breasts a horrible alarm bursts out, a cry

swelled by a fathomless panic:

"It's the insane train! The madman! On the ground! Help! On the ground! We're lost! Help! We're lost!"

Some type of gigantic, grey mass passes by—an ashen, misty mass with cut-out windows from end to end. One can feel the gust of a satanic draught from these open holes, hear the flapping, maddeningly blown-about shutters; one can almost see the spectral faces of the passengers....

Suddenly something strange occurs. The insane, rapacious train, instead of shattering its comrade, passes through it like a mist; for a moment one can see the fronts of the two trains go through each other, one can see the noiseless grazing of the coach walls, the paradoxical osmosis of gears and axles; one more second, and the intruder permeates with lightning fury through the train's solid body and disappears somewhere in the field on the other side. Everything quiets down....

On the track, before the station, the intact Brzesk passenger train stands peacefully. About it, a great bottomless silence. Only from the meadows, there in the distance, comes the low chirp of crickets, only along the wires above flows the gruff chat of the telegraph....

The people on the platform, the railwaymen, the clerks rub their eyes and look about in amazement.

Had what they seen really happened or was it just a strange hallucination?

Slowly, all eyes, united in the same impulse, turn towards the Brzesk train—it continues to stand silent and still. From inside, lamps burn with a steady, quiet light; at the open windows the breeze plays gently on the curtains.

A grave silence inhabits the cars; no one is disembarking, no one is leaning out from within. Through the illuminated quadrangle windows one can see the passengers: men, women, and children; everyone whole, uninjured—no one has received even the most minor contusion. Yet their state is strangely puzzling.

Everyone is in a standing position, facing the direction of

the vanished phantom locomotive. Some terrible force has bewitched these people, holding them in dumb amazement; some strong current has polarized this assembly of souls to one side. Their outstretched hands indicate some unknown goal, an aim surely distant; their inclined bodies lean to the distance, to a stunning, misty land far away; and their eyes, glazed by wild alarm and enchantment, are lost in boundless space.

So they stand and are silent; no muscle will twitch, no eyelid will fall. So they stand and are silent. . . .

Because through them has passed a most strange breath, because they have been touched by a great awakening, because they are already . . . insane. . . .

Suddenly strong and familiar sounds were heard, wrapped in the security of familiarity—strokes as firm as a heart when it beats against a healthy chest—steady sounds of habit, for years proclaiming the same thing.

"Ding-dong"—and a pause—"ding-dong . . . ding-dong . . ." The signals were operating. . . .

THE MOTION DEMON

The express Continental from Paris to Madrid rushed with all the force its pistons could muster. The hour was already late, the middle of the night; the weather was wet, showery. The beating rain lashed the brightly lit windows and was scattered on the glass in teary beads. Bathed in the downpour, the coaches glittered under roadside lamp-posts like wet armor, spewing sprightly water from their mouldings. A hollow groan issued forth into space from their black bodies, a confused chatter of wheels, jostling buffers, mercilessly trampled rails. Frenzied in its run, the chain of coaches awakened sleeping echoes in the quiet night, enticed dead voices along the woods, revived slumbering ponds. Some type of heavy, drowsy eyelids were raised, some large eyes opened in consternation, and so they remained in momentary fright. And the train sped on in a strong wind, in a dance of autumn leaves, pulling after it an extended swirling funnel of startled air, while smoke and soot clung lazily to its rear; the train rushed breathlessly on, hurling behind it the blood-red memory of sparks and coal refuse. . . .

In one of the first-class compartments, squeezed in the corner between the wall and an upholstered backrest, dozed a man in his forties of strong, Herculean build. The subdued lamplight that filtered with difficulty through the drawn shade lit up his long, carefully shaved face and revealed his firmly set, thin lips.

He was alone; no one interrupted his sleepy reveries. The quiet of the closed interior was disturbed only by the knocking of wheels under the floor or the flickering of gas in the gas-bracket. The red color of the plush cushions imbued a stuffy, sultry tone about the area that acted soporifically like a narcotic. The soft, yielding material muffled sounds, deadened the rattle of the rails, and surrendered in a submissive wave to the pressure of any weight. The compartment appeared to be plunged into deep sleep: the curtains drawn on ringlets lay dormant, the green net spread under the ceiling swung lethargically. Rocked by the car's steady motion, the traveller leaned his weary head on a headrest and slept. The book that had been in his hands slipped from his knees and fell to the floor. On a binding of delicate, dark-saffron skin the title was visible: *Crooked Lines*; near that, impressed with a stamp, the name of the book's owner: Tadeusz Szygon.

At some moment the sleeper stirred; he opened his eyes and swept them about his surroundings. For a second an expression of amazement was reflected on his face, and an effort at orientation. It seemed as if the traveller could not understand where he was and why he found himself there. But almost immediately a wry smile of forbearing resignation came to his lips. He raised his large, powerful hand in a gesture of surrender, and then an expression of dejection and contemptuous disdain passed over his face. He fell back into a half-sleepy state. . . .

Steps were heard in the corridor; the door was pulled back and a conductor entered the compartment.

"Ticket, please."

Szygon did not move a muscle; he showed no sign of life. Assuming he was asleep, the conductor came up and grasped him by the shoulder.

"Pardon me, sir; ticket, please."

With a faraway look in his eyes, the traveller glanced at the intruder.

"Ticket?" he yawned out casually. "I don't have one yet."

"Why didn't you buy it at the station?"

"I don't know."

"You're going to have to pay a fine."

"F-fine? Yes," he added, "I'll pay it."

"Where did you get on? Paris?"

"I don't know."

The conductor became indignant.

"What do you mean you don't know? You're making fun of me, my dear sir. Who should know?"

"It doesn't matter. Let's assume that I got on at Paris."

"And to what destination should I make the ticket out for?"

"As far as possible."

The conductor looked carefully at the passenger.

"I can only give you a ticket as far as Madrid; from there you can transfer to any train you like."

"It doesn't matter," replied Szygon with a disregardful wave of his hand. "As long as I just keep on riding."

"I will have to give you your ticket later. I must first draw it up and estimate the fine with the price."

"As you wish."

Szygon's attention suddenly became riveted by the railway insignias on the conductor's collar: several jagged little wings woven in a circle. As the sardonically smiling conductor was preparing to leave, Szygon sensed that he had already seen that face, twisted in a similar grimace, a few times before. Some fury tore him from his place, and he threw out a warning.

"Mr Wings, watch out for the draught!"

"Please be quiet; I'm closing the door."

"Watch out for the draught," Szygon repeated stubbornly. "One can sometimes break one's neck."

The conductor was already in the corridor.

"He's either crazy or drunk," he remarked under his breath, passing into the next car.

Szygon remained alone.

He was in one of his famous "flight" phases. On any given day, this strange person found himself, quite unexpectedly, several hundred miles from his native Warsaw and somewhere at the other end of Europe—in Paris, in London, or in some third-rate little town in Italy. He would wake up, to his extreme surprise, in an unknown hotel that he looked at for the first time in his life. How he came to be in such strange surroundings, he was never able to explain. The hotel staff, when questioned, generally measured the tall gentleman with a curious, sometimes sarcastic glance and informed him of the obvious state of things—that he had arrived the day before on the evening or morning train, had eaten supper, and ordered a room. One time some wit asked him if he also needed to be reminded under what name he had arrived. The malicious question was, after all, completely legitimate: a person who could forget what had occurred the previous day could also forget his own name. In any event, there was in Tadeusz Szygon's improvised rides a certain mysterious and unexplained feature: their aimlessness, which entailed a strange amnesia towards everything that had occurred from the moment of departure to the moment of arrival at an unknown location. This emphatically attested to the phenomenon being, at the very least, puzzling.

After his return from these adventurous excursions, life would go on as before. As before, he would ardently frequent the casino, lose his money at bridge, and make his renowned bets at horse races. Everything went along as it always had—normal, routine, and ordinary. Then, on a certain morning, Szygon would disappear once again, vanishing without a trace.

The reason for these flights was never made clear. In the opinion of some people, one had to look for its source in an atavistic element inherent in the nature of this eccentric; in Szygon's veins there apparently flowed Gypsy blood. It seemed he had inherited from his perpetually roaming ancestors a craving for constant roving, a hungry appetite for those sensations sought by these kings of the road. One example given as proof of this "nomadism" was the fact that Szygon could never reside long in any one place: he was continually changing his living quarters, moving from one section of town to the other.

Whatever impulses prompted his aimless romantic travels, he did not glory in them after his return. He would come back—likewise unexpectedly—angry, exhausted, and sullen. For the next few days he would lock himself in his home, clearly avoiding people, before whom he felt shame and embarrassment.

Most interesting of all was surely Szygon's state during these "flights"—a state almost completely dominated by subconscious elements.

Some dark force tore him from his home, propelled him to the railway station, pushed him into a carriage—some overpowering command impelled him, frequently in the middle of night, to leave his cozy bed, leading him like a condemned man through the labyrinth of streets, removing from his way a thousand obstacles, to place him in a compartment and send him out into the wide world. Then came a blindfolded, random journey, changing trains without any destination in mind, and a stop at some city or an out-of-the-way town or village, in some country, under some sky, not knowing why precisely there and not some other place—and finally a terrible awakening in unfamiliar, completely strange surroundings.

Szygon never arrived at the same place twice: the train always put him off at a different destination. During his ride he never "woke up," never became aware of the aimlessness of what he was doing—his full psychic faculties returned only after a conclusive departure from the train, and this frequently only after a deep, fortifying sleep in a hotel or a roadside shed or inn.

At the present moment he was in an almost trance-like state. The train now carrying him had departed yesterday morning from Paris. Whether he got on at the French capital or at some station along the road, he did not know. He had departed from somewhere and was now heading somewhere else—that was all he could say....

He adjusted himself on the cushions, stretched out his legs, and lit a cigar. He felt a sensation of distaste, almost repugnance. He always experienced similar feelings at the sight of a conductor or, for that matter, any railwayman. These people were a symbol of certain deficiencies or of an underdevelopment, and personified the imperfection that he saw in the railway system. Szygon understood that he made his unusual journeys under the influence of cosmic and elemental forces, and that train travel was a childish compromise caused by the circumstances of the terrain and his earthly environment. He realized only too well that if it were not for the sad fact that he was chained to the Earth and its laws, his travels, casting off the usual pattern and method, would take on an exceedingly more active and beautiful form.

It was precisely a train, the railway, and its employees that embodied for him that rigid formula, that vicious circle which he, a man, a poor son of the Earth, tried vainly to break out of.

That is why he despised these people; sometimes, he even hated them. This aversion to "servants of a charter for leisurely rambling," as he contemptuously called them, increased in direct proportion to his fantastic "flights," of which he was ashamed, not so much for their aimlessness but rather because they were conceived on such a pitiful scale.

This feeling of detestation was agitated by the little incidents and quarrels with the train authorities that were inevitable due to his unnatural state. On certain lines the employees already seemed to know him well, and during his journeys he would frequently detect the cruel smile of a porter, conductor, or railway official.

The conductor attending the coach he was now riding seemed to be particularly familiar. That lean, pitted face—lit up with a jeering little smile at the sight of him—had passed before his dreamy, faraway eyes not just once. At least, that is what he thought.

But most of all, Szygon was irritated by railway ads, publicity, and uniforms. How funny was the pathos of those travel allegories hanging about waiting rooms, how pretentious the sweeping gestures of those little geniuses of speed! Yet the most comical impression was created by those winged circles on the caps and lapels of the officials. What nerve! What fantasy! At the sight of these markings, Szygon frequently had the urge to tear them off and replace them with a likeness of a dog chasing its own tail. . . .

His cigar glowed peacefully, filling the compartment with small clouds of bluish smoke. Little by little the fingers holding the cigar loosened lazily and the fragrant Trabuco rolled under the seat, spattering a rocket of tiny sparks. Szygon fell asleep. . . .

A fresh release of steam in the pipes lisped quietly under his feet, spreading a pleasant, cozy warmth about the compartment. A mosquito, unusual for the season, hummed a faint song, made a few nervous circles, and hid itself in a dark recess among plush protuberances. And once again there was only the gentle flicker of the gas-burner and the rhythmic clatter of wheels. . . .

At some time during the night Szygon awoke. He rubbed his forehead, changed his sleeping position, and glanced about the compartment. To his surprise and displeasure he noticed that he was not alone: he had a travelling companion. Opposite him, spread out comfortably on the cushions, sat a railway official puffing on a cigarette and impertinently exhaling the smoke in his direction. Beneath this person's neglectfully unbuttoned jacket Szygon could see a velvet vest, and he was reminded of a certain stationmaster with whom he once had a fiery row. The railway official had, however, a familiar blood-red kerchief wrapped around his neck, just under a stiff collar with three stars and several winged circles, and this reminded Szygon of the insolent conductor who had irritated him earlier with his little smile.

"What the devil?!" he thought, carefully looking at the intruder's physiognomy. "Why, quite clearly it's the loathsome face of that conductor! The same emaciated, sunken cheeks, the same smallpox marks. But how did he get that rank and uniform?"

Meanwhile the "intruder" apparently noticed the interest of his fellow traveller. He let out a cone of smoke and, after lightly brushing ashes from his sleeve, put his hand to the peak of his cap and greeted him with a very sweet smile.

"Good evening!"

"Good evening," Szygon answered dryly.

"Have you been travelling far?"

"At the moment I'm not in a social mood. I generally like to travel in silence. That's why I usually choose a solitary compartment and pay a hefty gratuity for the pleasure."

Undeterred by the blunt retort, the railwayman smiled delightfully and continued with great composure:

"It doesn't matter. You'll slowly acquire the verve for speaking. It's just a question of practice and habit. Solitude is, as is known, a bad companion. Man is a social animal—*zoon politikon*—isn't that true?"

"If you want to consider yourself an animal, I personally have nothing against it. I am just a man."

"Excellent!" the official pronounced. "See how your tongue has loosened. It's not as bad as it seems. On the contrary, you possess a great talent for conversation, particularly in the direction of parrying questions. We'll slowly improve. Yes, yes," he added patronizingly, "somehow we'll make a go of it; somehow."

Szygon squinted his eyes suspiciously and studied the intruder.

After a moment of silence, the persistent railwayman continued: "Unless I'm mistaken we are old acquaintants. We've seen each other several times in the past."

Szygon's resistance slowly melted. The insolence of this person who insulted him with impunity, and for no apparent reason, disarmed him. He became interested in knowing more about this "stationmaster."

"It's possible," he said, after clearing his throat. "Only it seems to me that until recently you wore some other uniform."

At that moment a curious metamorphosis transformed the railwayman. The shirt with the glittering gold tinsel stars instantly disappeared, the red railway cap vanished, and now, instead of the kindly smiling stationmaster, the stooping, dishevelled, and sneering conductor, with his shabby jacket, and the ever-present bouquet of small lanterns attached to his person, sat opposite Szygon.

Szygon rubbed his eyes, involuntarily making a repelling

gesture.

"A transformation? Poof! Magic or what?!"

But already leaning towards him was the kindly "stationmaster," equipped with all the insignias of his office, while the conductor had hidden himself inside the uniform of a superior.

"Ah, yes," he replied casually, as if the process were nothing, "I've been promoted."

"I congratulate you," muttered Szygon, staring with amazement at the quick-change artist.

"Yes, yes," the other chatted away, "there 'above' they know how to value energy and efficiency. They recognize a good person: I've become a stationmaster. The railway, my dear sir, is a great thing. It is worthwhile to spend one's life in its service. A civilizing element! A swift go-between of nations, an exchange of cultures! Speed, my dear sir, speed and motion!"

Szygon disdainfully pursed his lips.

"Mr Stationmaster," he underlined scoffingly, "you're surely joking. What kind of motion? Under today's conditions, with improved technology, that excellent locomotive, the so-called 'Pacific Express' in America, runs at 200 kilometers an hour; if we grant in due time a further increase to 250 kilometers, even 300 kilometers—what of it? We are looking at an end result; despite everything, we haven't gone out even a millimeter beyond the Earth's sphere."

The stationmaster smiled, unconvinced. "What more do you want, sir? A wonderful velocity! 200 kilometers an hour! Long live the railway!"

"Have you gone crazy?" asked Szygon, already furious.

"Not at all. I gave a cheer to the honor of our winged patron. How can you be against that?"

"Even if you were able to attain a record 400 kilometers—what is that in the face of absolute motion?"

"What?" said the intruder, pricking up his ears. "I didn't quite get that—absolute motion?"

"What are all your rides, even with the greatest speed imaginable, even on the farthest extended lines, in comparison to absolute motion and the fact that, in the end, despite everything, you remain on the ground? Even if you could invent a devilish train that would circumvent the entire globe in one hour, eventually you'd return to the same point you started from: you are chained to the ground."

"Ha, ha!" scoffed the railwayman. "You are certainly a poet, my dear sir. You can't be serious?"

"What kind of influence can even the most terrific, fabulous speed of an earthly train have on absolute motion and its effect?"

"Ha, ha, ha!" bellowed the amused stationmaster.

"None!" shouted Szygon. "It won't change its absolute path by even an inch; it won't change its cosmic route even by a millimeter. We are riding on a globe turning in space."

"Like a fly on a rubber ball. Ha, ha, ha. What thoughts, what concepts! You are not only a first-class conversationalist, but a splendid humorist as well."

"Your pathetic train, your ant-like, frail train with its best, boldest 'speed,' as you like to term it, relies—notice, I'm clearly underlining this—relies simultaneously on twenty relative motions, of which every one on its own is by far stronger and unquestionably more powerful than your miniature momentum."

"Hmm ... interesting, most fascinating!" derided the unyielding opponent. "Twenty relative motions—a substantial number."

"I've omitted the incidental ones which for certain no railwayman has even dreamed of, and will mention the principal, pivotal ones known to every schoolboy. A train rushing with the greatest fury from A to B has simultaneously to make a complete rotation with the Earth round its axis in a twenty-four hour period. . . ."

"Ha, ha, ha! That's novel, absolutely novel."

"At the same time it whirls with the entire globe around the sun. . . ."

"Like a moth around a lamp."

"Spare me your jokes! They're not interesting. But that's not all. Together with the earth and the sun, the train goes along an elliptical line, relative to the constellation Centaurus, towards some unknown point in space to be found in the direction of the constellation Hercules."

"Philology at the service of astronomy. *Parbleu!* How profound!"

"You're an idiot, my dear sir! Let's move over to the incidental motions. Have you ever heard anything about the Earth's processional motion?"

"Maybe I've heard about it. But what does all this concern us? Long live the motion of a train!"

Szygon fell into a rage. He raised his mallet-like hand and let it drop forcefully on the scoffer's head. But his arm cut only through air: the intruder had vanished somewhere; the space opposite was suddenly vacant.

"Ha, ha, ha!" chortled someone from the other corner of the compartment.

Szygon turned around and spotted the "stationmaster" squatting between the headrest and the net; somehow he had contracted himself to a small size, and now looked like an imp.

"Ha, ha, ha! Well? Will we be civil in the future? If you want to talk further with me, then behave properly. Otherwise, I won't come down. A fist, my dear sir, is too ordinary an argument."

"For thick-headed opponents it's the only one; nothing else can be as persuasive."

"I've been listening," the other drawled, returning to his old place, "I've been listening patiently for a quarter of an hour to your utopian arguments. Now listen a little to me."

"Utopian?!" growled Szygon. "The motions I've mentioned are therefore fictitious?"

"I don't deny their existence. But of what concern are they to me? I'm only interested in the speed of my train. The only conclusive thing to me is the motion of engines. Why should I be concerned about how much forward I've moved in relation to interstellar space? One has to practical; I am a positivist, my dear sir."

"An argument worthy of a table leg. You must sleep well, Mr Stationmaster?"

"Thank you, yes. I sleep like a baby."

"Of course. That's easy to figure out. People like you are not tormented by the Motion Demon."

"Ha, ha, ha! The Motion Demon! You've fallen onto the gist of the matter! You've hit upon my profitable idea—actually, to tell the truth, not mine, but merely commissioned by me for a certain painter at our station."

"A profitable idea? Commissioned?"

"Oh, yes. It concerns a prospectus for a couple of new railway branches—the so-called *Veranuqunosbahnlinien*. Consider this—a type of publicity or poster that would encourage the public to use these new lines of communication. And so some vignette, some picture was needed, something like an allegory or symbol."

"Of motion?!" Szygon paled.

"Exactly. The aforementioned gentleman painted a mythical figure—a magnificent symbol that in no time swept through the waiting rooms of every station, not only in my country, but beyond its borders. And because I endeavored to get a patent and stipulated a copyright in the beginning, I haven't done badly."

Szygon raised himself from the cushions, straightening up to his full imposing height.

"And what figure did your symbol assume, if it's possible to know?" he hissed in a choked, strange voice.

"Ha, ha, ha! The figure of a genius of motion. A huge, swarthy young man balanced on extended raven wings, surrounded by a swirling, frenzied dance of planets—a demon of interplanetary gales, interstellar moon blizzards, wonderful, maddeningly hurling comets and more comets...."

"You're lying!" Szygon roared, throwing himself towards the speaker. "You're lying like a dog."

The "stationmaster" curled up, diminished in size, and vanished through the keyhole. Almost at the same moment the compartment door opened, and the disappearing intruder merged into the figure of the conductor, who was at the threshold. The conductor measured the perturbed passenger with a mocking glance and began to hand him a ticket.

"Your ticket is ready; the price, including the fine, is 200 francs."

But his smile was his ruin. Before he got a chance to figure out what was happening, some hand, strong like destiny, grabbed him by the chest and pulled him inside. A desperate cry for help was heard, then the cracking of bones. A dull silence followed.

After a moment, a large shadow moved along the windows of an empty corridor and towards the exit. Somebody opened the coach door and pulled the alarm signal. The train began to brake abruptly. . . .

The dark figure hurried down a couple of steps, leaned in the direction of the motion of the train, and with one leap jumped between roadside thickets glowing in dawn's light. . . .

The train halted. The uneasy crew searched long for the person who had pulled the alarm; it was not known from which coach the signal had originated. Finally the conductors noticed the absence of one of their colleagues. "Coach No. 532!" They rushed into the corridor and began to search through the cubicles. They found them empty, until in the last one, a first-class compartment at the end, they found the body of the unfortunate man. Some type of titanic force had twisted his head in such a hellish manner that his eyes had popped out of their sockets and were gazing at his own chest. Over the plucked whites, the morning sun played a cruel smile.

THE SLOVEN

After making the rounds of the coaches charged to his care, the old conductor, Blazek Boron, returned to the nook given over exclusively to his disposition, the so-called "place designated for the conductor."

Wearied by an entire day of tramping through the coaches, hoarse from calling out stations in the fog-swelled autumn season, he intended to rest a while on his narrow oilcloth-upholstered little chair; a well-earned siesta smiled worthily on him. Today's trip was actually over; the train had already made all its evenly distributed and short distance stops and was heading to the last station at a fast clip. Until the end of the trip Boron would not need to jump up from the bench and run through the coaches for several minutes to announce to the world, with a worn-out voice, that such and such station is here, that the train will stop for five minutes, ten minutes, or an entire lengthy quarter hour, or that the time has come to change trains.

He put out the lantern fastened to his chest and placed it high above his head on a shelf; he took off his greatcoat and hung it on a peg.

Twenty-four hours of continuous service had filled his time so tightly that he had eaten almost nothing. His body demanded its rights. Boron took out victuals from a bag and began to nourish himself. The conductor's grey, faded eyes settled on the coach window and he looked at the world beyond. The glass, rattling with the coach's tossing, was constantly smooth and black—he saw nothing.

He tore his eyes from the monotonous picture and directed them towards the corridor. His glance slid over the door leading to the compartments, went to the wall of windows opposite, and rested on the boring beaten pathway.

He finished his "supper" and lit a pipe. He was, in truth, still on the job, but in this area, particularly before the final destination, he did not fear the supervisor.

The tobacco was good, smuggled at the border; it smoked in circular, fragrant coils. From the conductor's lips spun out pliable ribbons and, twisting into balls of smoke, they rolled like billiard balls along the car corridor; in the next moment thick, dense spools unreeled from his lips to drift lazily upwards like blue stalks and crack like a petard at the ceiling. Boron was a master at smoking a pipe.

A wave of laughter flowed from the compartments: the guests were in a good mood.

The conductor tightened his teeth in anger; words of contempt fell from his lips.

"Commercial travellers! Tradesmen!"

Fundamentally, Boron couldn't stand passengers; their "practicality" irritated him. For him the railway existed for the railway, not for travellers. The job of the railway was not to transport people from place to place with the object of communication, but motion in and of itself, the conquest of space. Of what concern to it were the trivial affairs of earthly pigmies, the endeavors of industrial swindlers, the obscene allocations of tradesmen? Stations were present not to get off at, but to measure the distance passed; stops were the gauge of the ride, and their successive change, as in a kaleidoscope, evidence of progressive movement.

The conductor glanced with similar scorn at the throngs pressing through the car doors; he observed with a sardonic grimace the panting women and feverish-with-haste gentlemen pressing on heads, necks, amidst shouts, curses, sometimes jabs to get to the compartments to "occupy a place" and beat out their companions in the sheep-like run.

"A herd!" he spit out between his teeth. "As if the world depends on some Mr B. or some Mrs W. arriving 'in time' from F to Z."

Meantime, reality stood in striking contrast with Boron's views. People still got on and off at stations, still pushed with the same fierceness, and always for those same practical reasons. But the conductor also retaliated against this at every opportunity.

In his area, which took in three to four cars, it was never crowded, that horrible infliction of the mob that destroyed the will to live in his colleagues and was a dark stain on the horizon of a conductor's grey fate. What measures he used, what paths he took to reach this ideal, unrealized by others in his profession, no one knew. The fact remained that even in times of the greatest attendance, during the holidays, the interior of Boron's cars betrayed a normal look; the passageways were clear and in the lobbies one breathed in fairly good air. Supernumerary seating and "standing room only" spots the conductor did not accept. Severe with himself, fastidious in his job, he knew also how to be unyielding to travellers. Regulations he observed to the letter, at times with Draconian excess. Quibbling didn't help, ruses, swindles, or the deft slipping into the hand of a bribe—Boron could not be bought. He even took legal action against several people who tried this; one individual he slapped around for the insult, managing to get off lightly before the railway authorities when the matter was brought up before them. Sometimes it would happen that in the middle of the ride, somewhere on some squalid stop, on some miserable little station, in an open field, he would politely but firmly showed the door to a hoodwinking "guest."

Only twice in the course of his long career did he come upon "worthy" passengers who fulfilled his ideal of travellers to some extent.

One of these rare specimens was some nameless vagabond

who, without a penny to his name, had occupied a first-class compartment. When Boron demanded his ticket, the ragamuffin explained that he didn't need one because he was riding with no specific aim, just for the hell of it, from an innate necessity to move. The conductor not only acknowledged the reason, but also gave the compartment over to his exclusive use and took solicitous care of his guest's comfort for the entire journey. He even treated him to half of his provisions and lit a pipe with him amidst a friendly chat on the subject of travel as change.

The second similar passenger he met several years ago between Vienna and Trieste. He was an individual named Szygon, apparently a landowner from the Kingdom of Poland. This sympathetic person, besides being certainly rich, had also sat down in a first class compartment. Asked where he was going, he answered that in point of fact he himself didn't know where he got on, where he was bound for, and why.

"In that case," Boron remarked, "perhaps it would be best if you got off at the nearest station."

"Eh, no," countered the unique passenger, "I can't, upon my word, I can't. I have to go forward; something is driving me on. Draw up a ticket to wherever it pleases you."

The answer had charmed him to such a degree that he allowed the man to ride to the last station for free and didn't bother him any more. This Szygon apparently had the reputation of being a lunatic, but, according to Boron, if he was mad at all, then it was a madness with panache.

Yes, yes—there still existed in this wide world splendid travellers, but what were these rare pearls in an ocean of riff-raff? At times he would return with longing to these two wonderful incidents in his life, caressing his soul with the memory of exceptional moments. . . .

He inclined his head backwards and followed the movements of the blue-grey layers of pipe smoke hanging in the corridor. Above the rhythmic clatter of the rails was drawn out slowly the rapids of hot steam, driven through the pipes. He heard the gurgle of the water in the tank, he felt the warmth of its pressure along the edges of his utensils: the objects were warming up, for the evening was chilly.

The lamps at the top momentarily blinked their lighted eyelashes and died out. But not for long, for in the next moment the zealous regulator automatically injected a new dose of gas that fed the weakening burners. The conductor became aware of a specific, heavy scent, slightly reminiscent of fennel.

The smell was stronger than the pipe smoke, more pungent, and it clouded the senses.

Suddenly it seemed to Boron that he could hear the tread of bare feet along the corridor floor.

"Thud, thud, thud," the naked feet thumped. "Thud, thud, thud."

The conductor already knew what this meant; this was not the first time he had heard these steps in a train. He tilted his head and glanced into the dark car. There, at the end, where the wall broke off and retreated to the first-class compartments, he saw for a second his typically naked back—for a second that back flashed, taut as a bow and drenched in eyelash sweat.

Boron shuddered: The Sloven once again had turned up on a train.

He had noticed him the first time twenty years ago. It had been exactly an hour before the terrible catastrophe between Znicz and the Dukedom of Gaja, in which over forty people perished, not counting a great number of injured. The conductor was thirty-years old then and still strong-nerved. He remembered the details exactly, even the number of the unfortunate train. At the time he was conducting in the last cars and perhaps that is why he survived. Proud of his newly acquired promotion, he was taking home in one of the compartments his fiancée, his poor Kasienka, one of the victims of the disaster. In the middle of a conversation with her, he suddenly felt a strange unease: something was drawing him strongly out into the corridor. Unable to resist, he went out. At that moment he saw, at the exit of the car's vestibule, the vanishing figure of the naked giant; his body, grimed with soot, drenched in a sweat dirty from coal, gave off a stifling odor: there was in it the smell of fennel, the stench of burning smoke, and the scent of grease.

Boron threw himself after this figure, wanting to intercept him, but the vision vanished before his eyes. He merely heard for some time the thud of naked feet on the floor—thud, thud, thud—thud, thud, thud. . . .

Within an hour the train crashed into an express from the Dukedom of Gaja.

Since that time the Sloven had appeared before him two more times, each time as an announcement of a disaster. He saw him the second time several minutes before the derailment near Rawa. The Sloven was running on the car roofs and giving him signs with a stoker's cap that he had snatched off a sleepy head. He looked less threatening than on that first occasion. And somehow there had been no loss of life, merely a few minor injuries.

Five years later, riding the passenger train to Bazek, Boron saw him between two cars of a freight train heading in the opposite direction and bound for Wierszyniec. The Sloven was squatting on a buffer and playing with the chains. His colleagues laughed at him when he drew their attention to what he had seen, calling him crazy. But the near future proved him correct: that very night the freight train, going over a bridge, tumbled into a chasm.

The Sloven's omen was infallible: whenever he showed up, disaster was certain. These three experiences strengthened this conviction in Boron and shaped a deep belief connected with the Sloven's portentous appearance. The conductor felt a professional, idolatrous veneration towards him, and feared him as a deity of evil and menace. He surrounded this vision with a special cult; he formed an original view of this being.

The Sloven resided in the organism of a train, filling its multi-segmented frame, pounding unseen in the pistons, sweating in the locomotive boiler, tramping along the cars. Boron sensed his proximity—a presence permanent, continuous, albeit not visible. The Sloven lurked in the soul of a train; he was its mysterious potency during times of danger: at the moment of a bad presentment, he disengaged from it, thickened, and assumed corporeal form.

The conductor considered it needless, even laughable, to oppose him; any potential endeavors to ward off a disaster he foretold would be futile, obviously in vain. The Sloven was like fate. . . .

The renewed appearance of this oddity in the train, and right before the train's final destination, put Boron in a state of great excitement. At any moment one could expect an accident.

He got up and began walking nervously along the corridor. From one of the compartments came the hubbub of voices, the laughter of women. He came closer and looked inside for a few seconds. He dampened the gaiety.

A man drew back the door from a neighboring compartment and leaned out his head.

"Conductor, is it far to the station?"

"In half an hour we'll reach our goal. We're coming to the end."

Something in the intonation of the answer struck the questioner. His eyes paused for a long moment on the conductor. Boron smiled mysteriously and passed on. The head disappeared back inside.

Another man exited from a second-class compartment and, unlocking the corridor window, looked through it at the space beyond. His confused movements betrayed a certain unease. He raised the window and withdrew to the opposite side, to the end of the lobby. Here he dragged on a cigarette several times and, throwing glances at the butt, went out to the platform. Boron saw his silhouette leaning against the safety bar in the direction of travel.

"He's examining the area," he muttered, smiling maliciously. "Nothing will help. Accidents will happen."

Meanwhile the nervous passenger returned to the car. Spotting the conductor, he asked with forced calm: "Has our train already crossed with the express from Gron?"

"Not yet. We're expecting it at any moment. It's possible that we'll cross it at our final stop: it might be delayed. The express you're referring to is coming from an adjacent line."

At the moment, a loud rumble resounded from the right side. Beyond the window, a huge mass whisked by, belching flying sparks; after it, flashed a chain of black boxes lit up with cutout quadrangles. Boron pointed in the direction of the already disappearing train.

"That's it."

The uneasy gentleman, heaving out a sigh of relief, took out a cigarette and offered it to the conductor.

"Let's have a smoke. Genuine Phillip Morris."

Boron put his hand to the visor of his cap.

"Thank you very much. I only smoke a pipe."

"Too bad, because they're good."

The traveller lit up a cigarette by himself and returned to his compartment.

"Heh, heh, heh! He sensed something! Only he calmed down too quickly. Don't count your chickens before they're hatched."

But the successful crossing disturbed him a bit. The opportunity for an accident went down one degree.

It was already 9:45—in fifteen minutes they were scheduled to stop at Gron, the end of their ride. Along the way there was no bridge that could cave in; the only train coming from the opposite direction that they could have crashed into had been successfully passed. One should then expect a derailment or an accident at the station itself.

In any case, the Sloven's prognosis had to come true—he was bound to it, he, Boron, the old conductor.

This didn't concern the passengers, nor the train, nor his entire little self, but the infallibility of the barefooted oddity. Boron depended immensely on maintaining the Sloven's dignity against sceptical conductors, on preserving the Sloven's prestige in the eyes of unbelievers. The acquaintances to whom he had several times related the mysterious visits took the affair from a humouristic point of view, explaining the entire story as a hallucination, or, what was worse, the ramblings of someone who had drunk too much. This last conjecture hurt him especially, as he never imbibed in alcohol. Several railwaymen considered Boron a superstitious eccentric and not quite right in the head. Also called into play to a certain extent was his honor and healthy human reason. He would have preferred wringing his own neck than living through the Sloven's failure. . . .

In ten minutes it would be ten o'clock. He finished his pipe and went up some stairs to the top of the car, to a windowed cupola. From here, from the height of a crow's nest, the surrounding area lay during the day like the palm of one's hand. Now the world was plunged in dense darkness. Stains of light fell from the car windows, whose yellow eyes skimmed the embankment slopes. In front of him, at a distance of five cars, the engine sowed blood-red cascades of sparks, the chimney breathed out white-rose smoke. The black, twenty-jointed serpent glittered along its scaly sides, belched fire through its mouth, lit up the road with encompassing eyes. In the distance, the glow of a station was already visible.

As if sensing the nearness of the yearned-for stop, the train summoned all its strength and doubled its speed. Already the distance signal flashed phantom-like, set for clear passage, already semaphores were extending friendly arms in welcome. The rails started to duplicate, crossing in a hundred lines, angles, iron interweavings. As if in greeting, switch-signal lanterns to the right and left descended from the night shadows, station water-cranes, wells, heavy levers extended their necks.

Suddenly, several feet before the riotous locomotive, a red signal appeared. The engine threw out an abrupt whistle from its bronze throat, the brakes screeched, and the train, checked by the frenzied exertion of counter-steam, stopped right before the second switch signal.

Boron ran down and joined the flock of railwaymen who had gotten off to check the cause of the interruption in movement. The signal operator who had given the danger signal explained the situation. The first track, on which they were to ride, was temporarily occupied by a freight train. The switch had to be shifted and the train set onto the second track. Usually this manoeuvre is carried out at the signal-tower with the help of a lever. Meanwhile, however, the underground connection between it and the tracks had experienced some trouble, so the operator had to carry out the shifting outside with the aid of a key to get to the control switch.

The calmed crewmen returned to their cars to await the all-clear signal. Something riveted Boron in place. With a wandering gaze he looked at the blood-red signal, as if stupefied he listened to the grating sound of the rails shifting.

"At the last minute they discovered the problem! At almost the very last minute, some 300 meters before the station! So, was the Sloven lying?"

Suddenly he understood his role. He quickly advanced to the signal operator, who was now changing the color of the signal to green.

One had to divert this person from the switch at all cost and force him to leave his post.

Meanwhile, his comrades were already giving signs for movement. From the end of the train passed from lips to lips the cry: "All aboard!"

"Wait! Hold on!" Boron shouted.

"Signalman!" he said half-aloud to the railwayman, who then stood at attention. "I see some tramp in your tower."

The signal operator became alarmed. He strained his eyes in the direction of the little brick building.

"Hurry up!" insisted Boron. "Get going! He can play around with all the levers and upset the crossing!"

"All aboard! All aboard!" rang out the impatient voices of the conductors.

"Hold on, damn it!" protested Boron.

The signal operator, conquered by the power of the voice, the particular strength of the command, dashed towards the tower. Boron, taking advantage of this, grabbed the switch control and reversed it, connecting the rails to the first track.

The accomplished manoeuvre was deft, swift, and quiet. No one noticed.

"All aboard!" he shouted, withdrawing into the shadows.

The train moved, making up for time lost. In a moment the last car was already slipping into the semi-darkness, dragging after it a long trail of red lights. . . .

After a while, the confused signal operator ran up from the tower and looked carefully at the position of the switch control. He didn't like something. He raised a whistle to his lips and gave a three-tooted distress signal.

Too late! For a terrible crash from the station shook the air, a deafening, hollow boom of detonation, then a hellish racket, turmoil, and whining; wails, weeping, and screams were interwoven into a single wild chaos with the clash of chains, the cracking of shattering wheels, and the battering of mercilessly crushed cars.

"Collision!" murmured pale lips. "Collision!"

THE PERPETUAL PASSENGER

A small, nervous man in a threadbare coat, travelling suitcase in hand, forced his way through the crowds filling the station hall at Snowa. He seemed in a great hurry, elbowing roughly the peasant herds and throwing himself like a diver into the whirl of human bodies, as, from time to time, he fixed an uneasy glance at the clock reigning over the sea of heads.

It was already a quarter to four in the afternoon; in ten minutes the train for K. would be leaving. High time to buy a ticket and find a seat.

Finally, after superhuman exertions, Mr Agapit Kluczka forced his way through to the cashier area to stand in line and patiently wait his turn. But the slow movement forward, a step per minute, made him most restless, and soon those around him noticed a distressing tendency on his part to rush the travellers. Eventually, breathless, red like a beet, with drops of sweat covering his face, Kluczka reached the desired window. At this point, however, something unusual occurred. Instead of ordering a ticket, Kluczka opened his wallet, explored its interior, muttered something under his nose, and departed through the exit passage from the cashier.

One of the travellers, whose toe Kluczka had stepped on quite heavily during his trip to the window, noticed with no small indignation the whole puzzling manoeuvre and did not fail to be-rate him as he was leaving:

"You're crowding and pushing forward like a madman. One would think, God knows, that you're in a great hurry—and yet you leave the cashier without a ticket! Pooh! Crazy, crazy! Perhaps you left your house without taking any money?"

But Kluczka's mind was elsewhere. Having symbolically "acquired" a ticket, he rushed with a nervous step through the waiting room to the platform. Here, a throng of passengers was already awaiting the arrival of the train. Kluczka walked impatiently back and forth along the platform a couple of times, and then, offering an open cigarette case to a porter, asked:

"Is the train late?"

"Only by a quarter of an hour," the railwayman informed him, taking out with a smile a cigarette from the row offered him. "It should arrive in two minutes. So, sir, are you finally going to take your train ride to Kostrzan?" he asked, winking his eye playfully.

Kluczka became somewhat confused; his face reddened, and, turning on his heel, he trotted lightly beyond the second track. The porter, who knew him well, shook his head indulgently, waved his hand, and, taking his spot by the entrance to the waiting room, began to drag at his cigarette with pleasure.

Meanwhile, the train arrived. The wave of travellers swayed with unanimous rhythm, hurrying to the cars. So began a typical bousculade, the tripping over packages, the squeezing through the throngs—a crush, a hubbub, a tumult.

With the wild energy of an experienced player, Kluczka threw himself into the midst of the first line of attackers; along the way he knocked down a grey-haired old woman making her way to a compartment with two huge bundles; he toppled a nanny with an infant, and gave a black eye to some elegantly dressed gentleman. Unperturbed by the downpour of curses that fell upon him from the direction of his victims, Kluczka triumphantly entered onto the steps leading to a second-class car, and in one sprightly spring found himself in a long, narrow corridor. He wiped the sweat from his forehead, smiled victoriously, and glanced maliciously at the surging flocks of passengers below. But after five minutes of delight at being in an "occupied" space, he heard the whistle for departure and on his face a sudden transformation occurred: Kluczka became alarmed. And before the final response from a bugle, signalling departure, he grabbed his suitcase from the net, flashed like lightning by the backs of the amazed travellers, and got out through the back door facing the warehouses opposite the station.

At that moment, the train moved. Above Mr Kluczka's head the windows and the dark-green and black torsos of the cars began to pass by at an ever greater tempo; from one of the compartments the malicious head of some rascal leaned out, who, sighting the helpless standing man below, thumbed his nose derisively at him. Finally, the last car went by, and closing off the chain of its comrades with its wide, black back, it quickly slid out into the world. Kluczka looked for a moment with a plaintive glance at the disappearing train and lowered his suitcase sluggishly, in an intense image of resignation and grief. Then, under the crossfire of the ironical glances of the railroad functionaries, he dragged himself back to the waiting room.

Here the rows of waiting customers were dissipated; the main contingent had flowed out with train; the remaining passengers were waiting for a locomotive that ran on a side line, going south, in the direction of the mountains. There was plenty of time left: the next train was leaving after six in the evening.

Kluczka took a comfortable seat in the corner of the hall, blocked himself in with his suitcase, which he placed on the table opposite him, and taking out of his pocket a small packet, he started to partake of his modest afternoon snack. He felt comfortable in this snug nook, hidden in the darkness that was beginning to reach feebly into the hall here and there. He lazily straightened out his legs, leaned against the arm of the plush settee, and with complete pleasure gave himself over to absorbing the atmosphere of the waiting room and the station.

Mr Agapit Kluczka, by profession a judiciary clerk, was a passionate devotee of the railroad and travel. The environment of the railroad acted like a narcotic upon him, thrilling his entire being. The smell of smoke, locomotives, the sour scent of gas light, the specific stuffiness of the smoke and soot spilling out to the station corridors turned his head deliciously, dazed his consciousness and the clarity of his thinking. Had it not been for the wretched state of his health, he would have become a conductor so that he could ride continually from one end of the country to the other. He was immensely jealous of the constant vigor of railroad functionaries, that never-ending jumping from the train to the ground, from the ground to the train, riding and riding without a break until the day a wooden coffin would come. Unfortunately fate had rooted him to a little green table, tied him with a cord of boredom to piles of dust-covered deeds and papers. A law clerk. . . .

He glanced once again in the depths of his wallet and with a bitter smile slipped it back to his pocket.

"Thirty zlotys," he whispered out with a sigh, "and today is just the 5th. If it weren't for this cursed money situation, I could have been at Kostrzan before nightfall, together with all those lucky ones."

The thought of such an occurrence transferred him in one leap to the noisy environment of the Kostrzan station, plunging him into the tumult of voices, the chaos of signals, and the shiver of bells. From under his closed eyelids rolled out slowly two large silent tears that fell onto his short reddish moustache. . . .

Suddenly he came to. He rubbed his eyes quickly, twirled up his moustache, and straightening himself in the settee, he looked about the waiting room. He was met by the usual boredom of stations yawning with the contemplative grey monotony of repeated occurrences. The quiet of the hall was maybe broken from time to time by the dry cough of a consumptive, the heavy, traversing gait of a bored passenger, or the murmur of well-behaved children by the window asking something of their parents. The figures of the functionaries moved at times beyond the windows of the waiting room, or the red stain of a railway official's cap flitted by. Somewhere from a distance came the hysterical whistle of a soaring engine....

Kluczka focused his glance on the closest neighbor to his left, an old Jew—dozing in his gabardine for an hour in the same position.

"Going far?" he started the conversation.

The Jew, excavated from his sleepy meditations, looked at him reluctantly, drowsily.

"To Rajbrod," he yawned out, stroking his long ginger beard.

"So you're going south, towards the mountains. I'm also going in that direction. Beautiful scenery! Just ravines, forests, foothills. But one has to be very vigilant during the ride," he added, changing from an enthusiastic to a cautionary tone.

"And why is that?" asked the perturbed Jew.

"That region is a bit dangerous; you see, sir, there are always these forests, mountains, ravines. Apparently, from time to time, robbers turn up."

"Aj, aj," groaned out the Orthodox Jew.

"Well—not frequently—but caution can never hurt," calmed Kluczka. "It's best to ride in one of the middle cars and not inside a compartment but in the corridor."

"Why, sir?"

"It's easier to get out if something happens; a quicker means of escape. Through the window—hop!—into the fields, and you're gone!"

Kluczka brightened up considerably and, eyes sparkling with gusto, he started to unfold before his fellow passenger images of the potential dangers that could threaten travellers in that area. Kluczka was passing through a "warning phase," or, as he liked to call it, his "position as a danger signal." It was the first interlude, as it were, which was always played out in the waiting room, to which he returned after carrying out the first symbolic ride to K. Usually the victim of this ominous constellation of Kluczka's soul was the closest fellow traveller, male or female, who chanced to be in his proximity. Kluczka exerted himself into thinking of a thousand possible and impossible dangers, which he painted most artistically with the irresistible strength of his suggestion. And not just once would he get an unusual result. Several times after such a conversation some terrified Honourable Lady would cancel her trip, delaying it until "more peaceful times," or, if the ride was unavoidably necessary, with a devout sigh she would slip an envelope containing an offering inside the railway money box that bore the sign: "For a Safe Journey". . . .

The impulses that directed Kluczka in his warning phase were of a nature quite complex and unclear. Unquestionably, a certain role was played here by a desire of vengeance against the "lucky ones," as he called those travellers who were riding "in truth"—a desire deeply latent in his heart, one to which he would reluctantly have admitted; at the same time, other feelings were called into play, giving the entire tangle a special atmosphere. In spreading out before his victims' eyes the potential dangers of a train trip, Kluczka experienced together with them these intense experiences, attaining in this manner a surrogate perception of riding. Thus this warning phase was mixed in with his longings and impressions of travel, and train travel was his primary concern. . . .

The station clock tolled the sixth hour. In the hall movement started. Sleepy passengers leaned out from corners and, shaking off their drowsiness, they nervously grabbed their luggage, making their way to the glass doors leading to the platform.

Kluczka broke off in the middle of his sentence, adjusted his coat, straightened up, and with a bouncy step neared the departure gate. The porter retreated under the onrush of impatient customers, withdrawing to the depths of the platform. The crowds poured outside, carrying with them the already-irritated Kluczka. Shoving his way through the doors, Kluczka was met by the ironic glance of a functionary, but he pretended to be too distracted to notice.

"Damn it!" he thought, overtaking some gentleman. The train had already ridden up with bravado before the station, throwing lengthy white funnels of steam off to the sides.

Since the crush was less this time, Kluczka easily occupied an excellent first-class seat and settled comfortably in the red plush cushions. Because the train he was on crossed with the express from F., it stopped for a longer than usual length of time at Snowa, and Kluczka could surrender to the illusion of a symbolic ride in the direction of the mountains for a good half hour. But when the anticipated express flew by and disappeared in the distance in the midst of clouds of smoke, Kluczka imperceptibly took down his suitcase from the net and furtively slipped to the steps leading to the outside. When a minute later the departing wail of a bugle sounded, he ran unnoticed by anyone down the steps and found himself again in the waiting room. Along the way he once more paid off with a cigarette the porter, Wawrzyszyn, who was looking into his eyes a little insolently. In general, the poor wretch had to pay off the railroad service from time to time, so that it would look through its fingers at his caprices. He was well-known at the station under the nickname "the perpetual passenger" and also another, less flattering one, "the harmless madman."

Meanwhile the train departed and the second interval began. The waiting room had become deserted. The next passenger train in the direction of D. was due at ten at night; people weren't in a rush to get to the station.

The station was filled with late-afternoon boredom and reveries: grey spider threads began to spread along empty benches and yawn in recesses and corners. Under the ceiling of the hall roamed a few flies, buzzing monotonously, and with a strange stubbornness circling about a large, hanging chandelier. Outside the windows the first lights of switch signals flashed and bright streams from electric glass balls invaded the interior. In the dimness of the closed waiting room the solitary silhouette of the law clerk could be seen, somewhat hunched, bent, laid low to the ground. . . .

By the light from the platform, Kluczka studied a frayed old timetable; he searched out fictional train connections. Finally, his face flushed, he marked out most precisely the route that he promised to himself to carry out "in truth" around Easter when he would obtain a two-week vacation and a holiday supplement from his pension.

Finished with his calculations, he was looking one more time at his tiny, precise notations when the hall suddenly brightened up; from under the ceiling five electric bowls shot out their beams, from the walls jetted several light-yellow projections: the waiting room took on an evening atmosphere. The door handles of the nearby door moved to the inside and into the hall came several travellers. The previous mood was blown away irrevocably. Everything became bright as if in broad daylight.

Kluczka took his usual place of observation in the shadows of a heater; close by sat a woman of undetermined age. She seemed nervous, the corners of her mouth twitching and her movements fidgety. Kluczka felt very sorry for her all of a sudden and decided to calm his uneasy neighbor.

"Madam," he said, leaning to the lady and assuming an expression of near seraphic sweetness, "you must be completely surrendering to a traveller's mood?"

The woman, caught off guard, looked at him a little strangely.

"Madam," explained Kluczka in a silken voice, "you are simply suffering from the so-called 'railroad fever.' I am familiar with this, my dear lady, very familiar. Even though I am used to the railroad environment, I cannot master myself over it to this day. It constantly affects me with the same strength."

The woman looked at him kindly.

"To tell the truth, I do feel a little agitated; maybe not so much by the ride that awaits me, but by the uncertainty of how I'll manage after I arrive at my destination. I'm not familiar at all with the town I have to go to, I don't know to whom to turn, where to spend the night. I'm concerned about those first, exceedingly anxious moments immediately after one arrives."

Kluczka rubbed his hand in satisfaction: the lady simplified most wonderfully his passing over to the "information-clarification phase," which, in the progression of events, now appeared on the evening horizon. He drew out from a side pocket of his coat an impressive bundle of papers and notes, and spreading them out on the table, he turned with a friendly smile to his neighbor.

"Luckily I can be of service to you in the information you seek. Is it possible to know where madam is heading?"

"To Wyznia Retreat."

"Excellent. In a moment we'll know more about it. We'll take a look at the index in back of this station directory.... Wyznia Retreat.... Here it is! Line S-D, page 30. Splendid! ... Time of train departures: Passenger train at 4:30 at night, 11:20 before noon, and 10:03 in the evening. Cost of a second-class ticket, about 10.40. Let's go to the particulars of the locale. Wyznia Retreat—210 meters above sea level—a city of third-class size—20,000 inhabitants; under district law; a starosta, an elementary school, a secondary school..."

The lady interrupted his reading with an impatient motion of her hand.

"Hotels, my dear sir, are there any hotels?"

"Just one moment ... one moment and we'll find out.... Yes! Two inns, one eatery under the sign of 'The Cap of Invisibility' and the hotel 'Imperial'—here near the station to the right, two minutes away—sunny, large rooms starting from three kopeks up—excellent service, heating according to one's request, electricity, an elevator, steam bath below—a three minute leisurely, quiet walk away—dinner, supper, excellent home cooking. *Mein Liebchen, was ....*"

Kluczka bit his tongue, knowing that in the ardor of presenting this information, he had gone too far.

The lady beamed.

"Thank you, sir, thank you very much. Are you hired by this station as its information person?" she guessed, taking a purse out from her bag.

Kluczka became confused.

"Why, no, my dear lady. Please don't consider me an agent of the information bureau. I only do this as an amateur, from purely idealistic motives."

Once again the woman was seized by embarrassment.

"Excuse me, and once again a sincere thanks."

She gave him her hand, which he kissed chivalrously.

"Agapit Kluczka, judicial clerk," he presented himself, tipping his hat.

He was in a rosy mood. The information phase today had surpassed all his expectations so that when, around ten, the porter threw out in the hall with a stentorian voice the cry for departure, the perpetual passenger carried out all his symbolic actions with the redoubled energy of a young man in his twenties. And though after his repeated return to the waiting room, the third intermezzo did not seem tempting, his high enthusiasm did not fall, and Kluczka's spirit was bolstered with the memory of the successful information phase.

Despite this, today's "journey" was not fated to end happily. For when two hours later—that is, after midnight—Kluczka tried to force his way with his suitcase through the unprecedented crowds to a third-class compartment, he suddenly felt someone pluck him strongly by the collar and take him down roughly from the steps of the train. Looking around in fury, he saw by the light of a centre-track lantern the irate face of the conductor, and he heard in the tumult of voices the following apostrophe apparently meant for him:

"Get the hell out of here! There's a crush here so great that one can't even move a pin, and despite this, this lunatic is pushing through the steps like a madman and shoving people aside, only to jump out later on the other side at the moment of departure. I know you, my bird, and not just from today; I've been watching you for a long time! Well, get the hell out of here or I'll call the military police! There is no time today for indulging the halfwitted whims of crazy people!"

Stupefied, frightened to the bone, Kluczka found himself unexpectedly beyond the tight crowds of the passengers, and, as if drunk, he staggered somewhere among the columns of the platform.

"You deserved that," he murmured through tightened teeth. "Why did you have to push your way to the third-class compartment instead of the second? Inferior compartments, inferior service. I always told you that. One can tell a gentleman by his knee-boots."

Calmed a bit by this reasoning, he straightened his crumpled coat and went stealthily from the platform to the waiting room, from there to the entrance hall, and then to the street. He had had enough "travelling" for today—the last occurrence had disheartened him from finishing his journey, cutting it short by one hour.

It was already after midnight. The city slept. The lights of roadside inns had died out, beer houses and restaurants had become silent. Here and there a consumptive street lamp at a corner in the far distance brightened the darkness of the street; here and there, the faint gleam from some underground den slid along the sidewalk. Now and then, the quick step of a late passer-by, or the distant baying of dogs let down from a chain, interrupted the quiet of sleep....

With his suitcase in hand, the perpetual passenger dragged on slowly along a narrow winding street that crept somewhere among secluded lanes by the river. His head weighed like lead, his legs trod stiffly, wooden like crutch stilts. He was returning home for a few hours of sleep before daybreak, for tomorrow morning a desk was waiting for him, and after three o'clock, as today, as yesterday, as for many forgotten years, a symbolic journey.

IN THE COMPARTMENT

The train shot through the landscape as quick as a thought. Fields plunged into the darkness of evening, fallows bare and stark moved submissively behind, appearing like so many segments of a continuously folding fan. Taut telegraph wires went up, then went down, and once again unreeled along with perfect level straightness—stubborn, absurd, stiff lines.

Godziemba was looking through the coach window. His eyes, glued to the shiny rails, drank in their apparent movement; his hands, digging into the window sill, seemed to be helping the train push away the ground being passed. His heart rate was fast, as if wanting to increase the tempo of the ride, to double the momentum of the hollow-sounding wheels.

Winged with the rush of the locomotive, a bird flew easily from the fetters of commonplace existence and flashed by the lengthy coaches, brushing their windows in its exhilarated flight, and overtook the engine to soar to the wide, vanishing horizon, to a faraway, mist-covered world! . . . .

Godziemba was a fanatic of motion. This usually quiet and timid dreamer became unrecognizable the moment he mounted the steps of a train. Gone was the unease, gone the timidity, and the formerly passive, musing eyes took on a sparkle of energy and strength.

This notorious daydreamer and sluggard was suddenly transformed into a dynamic, strong-willed person with a feeling of self-worth. And when the lively bugle signal faded and the black coaches started towards their distant destinations, a boundless joy permeated his entire being, pouring warm and reviving currents into the farthest reaches of his soul, like the rays of the sun over the earth on summer days.

Something resided in the essence of a speeding train, something that galvanized Godziemba's weak nerves—stimulating strongly, though artificially, his faint life-force. A specific environment was created, a unique milieu of motion with its own laws and power, its own strange, at times dangerous, spirit. The motion of a locomotive was not just physically contagious; the momentum of an engine quickened his psychic pulse, it electrified his will—he became independent. "Train neurosis" seemed to transform temporarily this overly refined and sensitive individual into someone who exhibited a beneficial, positive force. His intensified excitement was maintained on an artificial summit above a frail life that, after the retreat of the "fortunate" circumstances, descended into a state of even deeper prostration. A train in motion affected him like morphine injected into the veins of an addict.

Finding himself in the four walls of a compartment, Godziemba became instantly enlivened. This misanthrope "on the mainland" threw off the skin of a recluse and initiated conversations with, at times, reluctant people; this taciturn and difficult man was suddenly transformed into a splendid conversationalist who showered his fellow travellers with anecdotes put together quickly in an adroit and witty manner. An oaf—who aside from his remarkable transformation aboard a train was undistinguished in everything else—became, from neither here nor there, a strong individual, venturesome and incisive. This chicken-hearted wallflower changed unexpectedly to a blustering brawler, who could even be dangerous.

Quite a few times during a ride Godziemba had gone through some interesting adventures, from which he emerged triumphant thanks to a pugnacious and unyielding attitude. A sarcastic witness to one such scene, who knew Godziemba well from another place, advised him to settle all his affairs of honor in a train—and one travelling at full speed at that.

"*Mon cher*, always duel in coaches; you'll fight like a lion. As God is my witness!"

But the artificial intensification of his life-force reverberated badly on his health: he paid the price for almost every ride with some illness. After each temporary increase of psychological powers an even more violent reaction would follow. Despite this, Godziemba liked riding trains immensely and repeatedly invented fictional travel goals just to opiate himself with motion.

So, yesterday evening, getting on the express at B., he really didn't know his purpose; he did not even reflect on what he would do tonight at F., where in a few hours the train would deposit him. All this was of little consequence. What did it matter to him? For here he sits comfortably in a warm compartment, looking through the window at the landscape whisking by, and he is riding at a speed of 100 kilometers an hour. . . .

Meanwhile, outside it had darkened completely. A lamp near the ceiling, turned on by an unseen hand, vividly lit up the interior. Godziemba drew the curtain, turned his back to the window, and glanced at the compartment. Having been engrossed with the murky countryside, he had not noticed that at one of the stations two people had entered his compartment to occupy the empty seats opposite him.

Now in the lamp's yellow light he saw his fellow passengers. They were probably newly-weds. The man, tall, lean, with dark blond hair and a clipped moustache, appeared to be in his thirties. Bright, cheerful eyes looked out from under his heavily defined brows. The sincere, somewhat long face was enhanced by a pleasant smile whenever he would turn to his companion.

The woman, also blonde but with a lighter hue, was small but very well developed. Her luxuriant hair, twisted unpretentiously in two thick braids at the back of her head, framed a face that was delicate, fresh, and attractive. The short grey petticoat, clasped simply with a leather belt, emphasized the alluring curves of her hips and firm, young breasts.

Both travellers were covered heavily with the dust and dirt of the roads; they were apparently returning from an outing. An aura of youth and health came from them—that refreshing vigor which mountain climbing gives to tourists. They were occupied in a lively conversation. It seemed they were sharing impressions of their excursion, for the first words Godziemba heard referred to some uncomfortable summit hostel.

"It's a pity we didn't take that woollen blanket with us; you know, the one with the red stripes," said the young lady. "It was a bit too cold."

"Shame on you, Nuna," scolded her companion with a smile. "One shouldn't admit to being so weak. Do you have my cigarette case?"

Nuna plunged her hand into the travelling bag and withdrew the requested article.

"Here, but I think it's empty."

"Let me see."

He opened it. His face registered the disappointment of a passionate smoker.

"Too bad."

Godziemba, who had managed several times to catch the glance of the vivacious blonde, took advantage of the opportunity and, removing his hat, politely offered his abundantly-filled cigarette case.

"Can I be of service?"

Returning his bow, the other man drew out a cigar.

"A thousand thanks. An impressive arsenal! Battery beside battery. You are more far-sighted than I, sir. Next time I'll supply myself better for the road."

The preliminaries were successfully passed; a leisurely conversation commenced, flowing along smooth, wide channels.

The Rastawieckis were returning from the mountains after

an eight-day excursion made partly on foot, partly on bicycles. Twice rain had drenched them in the ravines; once they had lost their way in some dead-end gully. Despite this, they ultimately overcame their difficulties, and the vacation had turned out splendidly. Now they were returning by train, soundly tired but in excellent humour. They might have had one more week of fun among the ranges of the East Beskids if not for the engineer's surveying job. Anticipating an avalanche of work in the near future, Rastawiecki was taking just this short break. He was going back gladly, for he liked his work.

Godziemba listened only casually to these explanations, divided between the engineer and his wife; instead, he was taken up with Nuna's physical allurements.

One couldn't call her beautiful; she was just very pleasant and maddeningly enticing. Her plump, slightly stocky body exuded health and freshness, and aroused his libido with its seductive scents of wild herbs and thyme.

From the moment he saw her large blue eyes, he felt an irresistible attraction. This was odd, for she did not fit his ideal. He preferred brunettes by far, with slender waists and Roman profiles. Nuna belonged to the exact opposite type. Besides, Godziemba did not get excited easily; he was by nature rather cool, and in sexual relations abstinent.

Yet all it took was a meeting of their eyes to kindle a secret fire of lust within him.

So he looked at her intensely; he followed her every movement, her every change in position.

Had she noticed anything? Once he caught an embarrassed glance thrown furtively from under her silky eyebrows—and he also thought he had detected on her luscious cherry lips a little smile full of coquetry and pleased pride meant for him.

This stimulated him. He became daring. During the conversation he moved slowly away from the window and shifted imperceptibly closer to her knees. He felt them opposite his and their pleasant warmth radiating through the grey, woollen dress.

Then, when the coach gave a slight tilt at a turn, their knees met. For a few seconds he drank in the sweetness of the touch. He pressed harder, nestled there, and, with inexpressible joy, felt he was being similarly answered. Was this an accident?

No. Nuna didn't withdraw her legs; on the contrary, she crossed one over the other in such a manner that her slightly raised thigh hid Godziemba's slightly too persistent knee from her husband. In this manner, they rode for a long, exquisite time. . . .

Godziemba was in an excellent mood. He told jokes and wicked witticisms that were, however, still acceptable in polite company. The engineer's wife continually burst out with ripples of silvery laughter, revealing in sparkling profusion, a little predatorily, her even, shiny teeth. The movement of her rounded hips, shaking with shivers of laughter, was soft, feline, almost lascivious.

Godziemba's cheeks became flushed, his eyes sparkled with fire and intoxication. An overpowering aura of lust exuded from him, forcefully drawing the engineer's wife into his bewitching sphere.

Rastawiecki divided his gaiety among them. Some peculiar blindness threw an ever-thicker curtain over the duplicitous behavior of his companion, some strange indulgence made him look through his fingers at his wife's deportment. Perhaps he never had a reason to be suspicious of Nuna's frivolousness, and that was why he acted thus. Perhaps he did not yet know the sex demon, suppressed under superficial domesticity, and had never been aware of its corrupting influence and deceitfulness. A fatal spell enfolded these three people in its domain and drove them towards frenzy and abandonment—one saw it in the spasmodic movements of Nuna's body, the blood-shot eyes of her admirer, the sardonic grimace of the husband's lips.

"Ha, ha, ha!" laughed Godziemba.

"Hi, hi, hi!" seconded the woman.

"He, he, he!" responded the engineer.

And the train rushed breathlessly along; it darted up hills, slid down valleys; it ripped up the landscape with its powerful chest. Rails rattled, wheels rumbled. . . .

Around one o'clock Nuna began to complain of a headache; the lamp's bright light bothered her. The obliging Godziemba let down the shade over it. From then on, they rode in semi-darkness.

The mood for conversation slowly died out. The words fell infrequently, interrupted by the yawning of the engineer's wife; the lady was apparently sleepy. She tilted her head backwards, leaning it against her husband's shoulder. But the legs that were carelessly stretched out towards the opposite seat did not lose contact with her neighbor; on the contrary, now, in the darkened atmosphere, they were considerably more unrestrained. Godziemba felt them continually, as their sweet weight exerted an inert pressure on his shin bone.

Rastawiecki, wearied by travel, hung his head on his chest. Sinking between the plush cushions, he fell asleep. Shortly, in the quiet of the compartment, one could hear his even, calm breathing. Silence prevailed. . . .

Godziemba was not asleep. Stimulated erotically, burning like iron in a fire, he merely closed his eyelids in pretence. Hot currents of strongly pulsating blood coursed through his body; a delicious lethargy unravelled the elasticity of his limbs, lust's lassitude took control of his mind.

He delicately placed his hand on Nuna's leg and felt her firm flesh with his fingers. A sweet giddiness misted his eyes. He moved his hand higher, imagining the silky touch of her body. . . .

Suddenly her hips undulated with a shiver of pleasure; she stretched out her hand and plunged it into his hair. The silent caress lasted but a moment. . . .

He raised his head and met the moist glance of her passionate eyes. With her finger she indicated the second half of the compartment, even darker than where they were. He understood. He got up, slid past the sleeping engineer, and, tiptoeing, went to the other half of the compartment. Here, covered by dense obscurity and a partition that reached his chest, he sat down in excited anticipation.

But the rustling that had occurred, despite all caution, woke up Rastawiecki. He rubbed his eyes and glanced around. Nuna, nestling down momentarily in the corner of the compartment, pretended to be dozing. The place opposite him was empty.

The engineer yawned slowly and straightened up.

"Quiet, Mieciek," she reprimanded him with a sleepy pout. "It's late."

"Sorry. Where is that—satyr?"

"What satyr?"

"I dreamt of a satyr who had the face of that gentleman who was sitting opposite us."

"He probably got off at some station. Now you have the space to yourself. Get comfortable and go to sleep. I'm tired."

"Good advice."

He yawned again, stretched himself out on the oilcloth cushions, and placed an overcoat under his head.

"Good night, Nuna."

"Good night."

Silence fell.

With bated breath, Godziemba had been crouching behind the partition during this brief scene, waiting for the dangerous moment to pass. From his dark corner, he saw only the engineer's empty, still boots projecting beyond the edge of the bench, and, on the opposite seat, Nuna's grey silhouette. Mrs Rastawiecki remained in the same position as her husband had found her after his awakening. But her open eyes glowed in the semi-darkness hungrily, wildly, provocatively. Thus passed fifteen minutes of travelling.

Suddenly, against the background of the rattling of the coach, sharp snoring sounds came from the engineer's open mouth. Rastawiecki was asleep for good. Then, nimble like a cat, his wife got off the cushions and found herself in Godziemba's arms. With a silent but powerful kiss they connected their craving lips and became entangled in a long, hungry embrace. Her young, robust breasts pressed burningly against him, and she gave him the fragrant conch of her body. . . .

Godziemba took her. He took her like a flame in the swelter of a conflagration that destroys and consumes and burns; he took her like a gale in unbridled, unrestrained frenzy, a savage wind of the steppe. Dormant lust exploded with a red cry and tore at the bit. Pleasure, bridled at first by fear and the affectation of prudence, finally broke out triumphantly in a rich scarlet wave.

Nuna writhed in passion; she bucked with spasms of boundless love and pain. Her body, bathed in mountain streams, swarthy from the winds of mountain pastures, smelled of herbs thick, raw, and giddy. Her young vaulted hips, soft at the buttocks, were opening up like private tufts of a rose, and they drank and sucked in love tribute. Freed from binding clips, her flaxen hair fell smoothly over her shoulders and enclosed him. Sobs shook her chest, her parched lips threw out some words and entreaties.

Suddenly Godziemba felt a tangible pain at the back of his head, and almost simultaneously he heard Nuna's distressed cry. Half-conscious, he turned around and at the same time received a strong blow on his cheek. Blood rushed to his head, fury twisted his lips. Like lightning he countered the next intended punch as his fist smashed his opponent between the eyes. Rastawiecki reeled, but did not fall down. A fierce fight commenced in the semi-darkness.

The engineer was a tall, strong man, yet the frenzy of victory immediately tilted towards Godziemba. In this individual, by all appearances slender and weak, some feverish, pronounced strength had been awakened. An evil, demonic strength raised his frail arms, inflicted blows, neutralized the attack. Wild, bloodshot eyes predatorily watched the enemy's movements, they read his thoughts, anticipated his intentions.

The two men struggled in the quiet of a night disrupted by the rumble of the train, the noise of their feet, or the quick breathing of overworked lungs. They struggled in silence like two boars fighting over a female, who was cuddled in the niche of the compartment.

Because of the tight confines, the fight was restricted to an extremely narrow area between the seats, moving from one part of the compartment to the other. Gradually the opponents tired each other out. Big drops of sweat flowed down from exhausted foreheads; hands, weak from punching, were lifted up ever more heavily. Already Godziemba had stumbled onto the cushions from a well-measured push; but in the next second he was up. Gathering his remaining strength, he used his knee to thrust away his opponent; then with enraged momentum he threw him to the opposite corner of the compartment. The engineer staggered like a drunk, the weight of his body broke open the door. Before he got a chance to stand up, Godziemba was shoving him towards the platform. Here was played out the final short and relentless act of the battle.

The engineer defended himself weakly, parrying with difficulty his opponent's frenzied fury. Blood was running down his forehead, lips, nose; it was pouring over his eyes.

Suddenly Godziemba rammed into him with the full weight of his body. Rastawiecki lost his balance, reeled, and fell under the wheels of the train. His hoarse scream drowned out the groan of the rails and the rumble of the coaches. . . .

The victor breathed freely. He drew the cool night air into his exhausted chest, rubbed the sweat from his forehead, and straightened his crumpled clothes. The draught of the rushing train streamed through his hair and cooled his hot blood. He took out his cigarette case and lit up a smoke. He felt somehow refreshed, happy.

He calmly opened the door that had slammed shut during the fight, and with a sure step returned to the compartment. As he entered, warm, serpentine arms embraced him. In her eyes glowed the question:

"Where is he? Where is my husband?"

"He will never return," he answered indifferently.

She cuddled against him.

"You will protect me from the world. My beloved!"

He embraced her strongly.

"I don't know what is happening to me," she whispered, leaning against his chest. "I feel such a sweet giddiness in my head. We've committed a great sin, but I'm not afraid beside you, my strength. Poor Mieciek! . . . You know it's terrible, but I'm not sorry for him. Why, that's horrible! He's my husband!"

She drew back suddenly, but looking into his eyes, intoxicated with the fire of love, she forgot everything. They started to devise plans for the future. Godziemba was a rich man and of independent means—no occupation tied him down, he could leave the country at any time and take up residence anywhere in the world. So, they will get off at the nearest station, where the rail lines cross, and go south. The connection will be excellent—the express to Trieste departs at daybreak. He'll buy the tickets immediately, and in twelve hours they'll reach the port. From there, a ship will take them to a land of oranges where a May sun sweetens trees, where the ocean's deep-blue chest washes golden sand, and a pagan god's forest crowns the head with laurel wreaths.

He spoke in a calm voice, sure of his manly aims, indifferent towards the judgment of people. Brimming with energy, ready to contend with the world, he lifted her collapsing figure.

Nuna, who had been listening intently to the sound of his words, appeared to be dreaming some strange, singular fairy tale, some golden, wonderful story. . . .

The engine's loud whistle announced the station. Godziemba trembled.

"It's time. Let's get our things together."

She got up and took down her travel coat from the overhanging net. He helped her dress.

Streaks of the station's lamplights fell through their window. A protracted shudder once again shook Godziemba.

The train stopped. They left the compartment and descended to the station platform. They were swept up and absorbed by the multitude, by the tumult of voices and lights.

Suddenly, Nuna, leaning on his arm, weighed heavily on him like fate. In the twinkling of an eye, somewhere from the corner of his soul, dread crept in, an insane dread, and it made his hair stand on end. A feverishly drawn mouth cried out the danger. Horrible, base fear bared its sharp claws.

He was just a murderer and a despicable coward.

In the midst of the greatest throng, he freed his arm from Nuna's embrace, stepped away from her without being noticed, and made his way through some dark corridor to the outside of the station. A maddened flight ensued along the back-streets of an unknown city. . . .

SIGNALS

At the depot station, in an old postal car taken out of service long ago, several off-duty railwaymen were gathered for their usual chat: three train conductors, the old ticket collector, Trzpien, and the assistant stationmaster, Haszczyc.

Because the October night was rather chilly, they had lit a fire in a little iron stove whose pipe exited out of an opening in the roof. The group was indebted for this happy idea to the inventiveness of the conductor, Swita, who had personally brought over the rust-corroded heater, discarded from some waiting room, to adapt it so splendidly to the changed circumstances. Four wooden benches, their oilcloth covering torn, and a three-legged garden table, wide like a record turntable, completed the interior furnishings. A lantern, hanging on a hook above the heads of those who sat below, spread out along their faces a hazy, semi-obscure light.

So looked the "train casino" of the Przelecz station officials, an improvised refuge for homeless bachelors, a quiet, secluded stop for off-duty conductors. Here, in their spare moments, zapped of energy by their riding patrons, the old, grey "train wolves" converged to relax after the executed tour, and chat with professional comrades. Here, in the fumes of conductors' pipes, the tobacco smoke, the cigarettes, and cuds of chewing tobacco, wandered the echoes of tales, thousands of adventures and anecdotes: here spun out the yarn of a railwayman's fate.

And today the noisy meeting was also animated, the group exceptionally well-suited, just the cream of the station. A moment ago Trzpien had related an interesting episode from his own life and had managed to rivet the attention of his audience to such a degree that they forgot to feed their dying-out pipes, and they now held them in their teeth already cold and extinguished like cooled-down volcano craters.

Silence filled the car. Through the window, damp from the drizzle outside, one could see the wet roofs of train cars, shiny like steel armor under the light of reflectors. From time to time the lantern of a trackwalker flashed by, or the blue signal of a switching engine; from time to time the green reflection of the switch signal ploughed through the darkness, or the penetrating call of a trolley was heard. From afar, beyond the black entrenchment of slumbering cars, came the muffled buzz of the main station.

Through the gap between the cars, a portion of track was visible: several parallel strips of rail. On one of them an empty train slowly pulled in; its pistons, tired by a full day's race, operated sluggishly, transforming their motion to the rotations of the wheels.

At a certain moment the locomotive stopped. Under the chest of the machine whirls of vapors emerged, enfolding the rotund framework. The lantern lights at the front of the colossus began to bend in rainbow-colored aureoles and golden rings, and became enveloped with a cloud of steam. Then came an optical illusion: the locomotive and, with it, the cars, rose above the layers of steam and remained suspended in the air. After several seconds the train returned to the rails, emitting from its organism the last puffs, to plunge itself into the reverie of a nightly repose.

"A beautiful illusion," remarked Swita, who had been looking for a long time through the window pane. "Did all of you see that apparent levitation?"

"Certainly," confirmed several voices.

"It reminded me of a rail legend I heard years ago."

"Tell us about it, Swita!" exhorted Haszczyc.

"Yes, go on!"

"Of course—the story isn't long; one can sum it up in a couple of words. There circulates among railwaymen a tale of a train that disappeared."

"What do you mean 'disappeared'? Did it evaporate or what?"

"Well, no. It disappeared—that doesn't mean that it stopped existing! It disappeared—that means its outward appearance is not to be seen by the human eye. In reality, it exists somewhere. Somewhere it dwells, though it's not known where. This phenomenon was supposed to have been created by a certain stationmaster, some real character and maybe even a sorcerer. This trick was performed by a series of specially arranged signals that followed each other. The occurrence caught him off guard, as he later maintained. He had been playing around with the signals, which he had arranged in the most varied ways, changing their progression and quality; until one time, after letting out seven of such signs, the train driving up to his station suddenly, at full speed, rose parallel to the track, wavered a few times in the air, and then, tipping at an angle, vanished. Since that time no one has seen either the train or the people who were riding in it. They say that the train will appear again when someone gives the same signals but in the reverse order. Unfortunately the stationmaster went insane shortly thereafter, and all attempts to extract the truth from him proved abortive. The madman took the key to the secret with him when he died. Most probably someone will hit upon the right signs by accident and draw out the train from the fourth dimension to the earth."

"A real fuss," remarked Zdanski, a train conductor. "And when did this wonderful event occur? Does the legend fix a date for it?"

"Some hundred years ago."

"Well, well. A pretty long time! In that case the passengers inside the train would be, at the present moment, older by an entire century. Please try and imagine what a spectacle it would be if today or tomorrow some lucky person were able to uncover the apocalyptic signals and remove the seven magical charms. From neither here nor there the missing train suddenly falls from the sky, suitably rested after a hundred-year hoisting, and throngs pour out stooping under the burden of a century of existence!"

"You forget that in the fourth dimension people apparently do not need to eat or drink, and they don't age."

"That's right," declared Haszczyc, "that's absolutely right. A beautiful legend, my friend, very beautiful."

Remembering something, he became silent. After a moment, referring to what Swita had related, he said thoughtfully:

"Signals, signals. . . . I've something to say about them—only it's not a legend, but a true story."

"We're listening! Please, go ahead!" echoed back a chorus of railwaymen.

Haszczyc rested an elbow against the table top, filled his pipe, and, expelling a couple of milky spirals, began his story:

One evening, around seven o'clock, an alarm went out to the Dabrowa station with the signal "cars unattached." The hammer of the bell gave off four strokes by four strokes spaced apart by three seconds. Before Stationmaster Pomian could figure out from where the signal originated, a new signal flowed from the region. Three strikes alternating with two, repeated four times, could be heard. The official understood: they meant "stop all trains." Apparently the danger had increased.

Moving along the track slope and in the direction of a strong westerly wind, the detached cars were running towards the passenger train leaving the station at that moment.

It was necessary to stop the passenger train and back it up several kilometers and somehow cover the suspected part of the region.

The energetic young official gave the suitable orders. The passenger train was successfully turned back from its course and at the same time an engine was sent out with people whose job was to stop the racing separated cars. The locomotive moved carefully in the direction of danger, lighting up the way with three huge reflectors. Before it, at a distance of 700 meters, went two trackwalkers with lighted torches, examining the line attentively.

But to the amazement of the entire group, the runaway cars were not met with along the way, and, after a two-hour inspection to the end of the ride, the engine turned back to the nearest station at Glaszow. There, the stationmaster received the expedition with great surprise. Nobody knew anything about any signals, the region was absolutely clear, and no danger threatened from this side. The officials, worn-out by tracking, got on the engine and returned to Dabrowa near eleven at night.

Here, meanwhile, the unease had increased. Ten minutes before the engine's return, the bell sounded again, this time demanding the sending of a rescue locomotive with workers. The stationmaster was in despair. Agitated by the signals continually flowing from the direction of Glaszow, he was pacing restlessly about the platform, going out to the line to return again to the station office baffled, terrified, frightened.

In reality, it was a sorry situation. His comrade from Glaszow, alarmed by him every dozen or so minutes, answered at first with calm that everything was in order; later, losing his patience, he started to scold fools and lunatics. To Dabrowa, meanwhile, came signal after signal, entreating ever more urgently the dispatching of workers' cars.

Clinging on to the last plank like a drowning man, Pomian phoned the Zbaszyn station, in the opposite direction, supposing, he didn't know why, that the alarm was coming from there. Naturally he was answered in the negative; everything was in perfect order in that area.

"Have I gone crazy or is everyone not in their right minds?" he finally asked a passing blockman. "Mr Sroka, have you heard these damned bell signals?"

"Yes, stationmaster, I heard them. There they go again! What the hell?"

Indeed, the relentless hammer struck the iron bell anew; it called for help from workers and doctors.

The clock already read past one.

Pomian flew into a rage.

"What business is this of mine? In this direction, everything's fine, in that direction, everything's in order—then what the hell do they want? Some joker is playing games with us, throwing the whole station upside-down! I'll make a report—and that's that!"

"I don't think so, stationmaster," his assistant calmly put in; "the affair is too serious to be grasped from this point of view. One rather has to accept a mistake."

"Some mistake! Haven't you heard, my friend, the answer from both of the stations nearest to us? It's not possible that these stations would not have heard any accidentally stray signals from stops beyond them. If these signals reached us, they would have to go through their regions first! Well?"

"So the simple conclusion is that these signals are coming from some trackwalker's booth between Dabrowa and Glaszow."

Pomian glanced at his subordinate attentively.

"From one of those booths, you say? Hmm . . . maybe. But why? For what purpose? Our people examined the entire line, step by step, and they didn't find anything suspicious."

The official spread out his arms.

"That I don't know. We can investigate this later in conjunction with Glaszow. In any case, I believe we can sleep peacefully tonight and ignore the signals. Everything that we had to do, we did—the region has been searched rigorously, on the line there isn't any trace of the danger we were warned about. I consider these signals as simply a so-called 'false alarm.'"

The assistant's calmness transferred itself soothingly to the stationmaster. He bid him leave and shut himself in his office for the rest of the night.

But the station personnel did not ignore this so easily. They gathered on the block around the switchman, whispering secretively among themselves. From time to time, when the quiet of the night was interrupted by a new ringing of the bell, the heads of the railwaymen, bent towards each other, turned in the direction of the signal post, and several pairs of eyes, wide with superstitious fear, observed the movements of the forged hammer.

"A bad sign," murmured Grzela, the watchman; "a bad sign!"

Thus the signals played on until the start of daybreak. But the closer morning came, the weaker and less distinct the sounds; then long gaps between each signal ensued, until the signals died down, leaving no trace at dawn. People sighed out, as if a nightmarish weight had been lifted from their chests.

That day Pomian turned to the authorities at Ostoi, giving a precise report of the occurrences of the preceding night. A telegraphed reply ordered him to await the arrival of a special commission that would examine the affair thoroughly.

During the day, the rail traffic proceeded normally and without a hitch. But when the clock struck seven in the evening, the alarm signals arrived once again, in the same succession as the night before. So, first came the "cars unattached" signal; then the order "stop all trains"; finally the command "send a locomotive with workers" and the distress call for help, "send an engine with workers and a doctor." The progressive excellence of the signals was characteristic; each new one presented an increase in the fictitious danger. The signals clearly complemented each other, forming, in distinctive punctuations, a chain that spun out an ominous story of some presumed accident.

And yet the affair seemed like a joke or a silly prank.

The stationmaster raged on, while the personnel behaved variously; some took the affair from a humorous point of view, laughing at the frantic signals, others crossed themselves superstitiously. Zdun, the blockman, maintained half-aloud that the devil was sitting inside the signal post and striking the bell out of contrariness.

In any event, no one took the signals seriously, and no

suitable orders were given at the station. The alarm lasted, with breaks, until the morning, and only when a pale-yellow line cut through in the East did the bell quiet down.

Finally, after a sleepless night, the stationmaster saw the arrival of the commission around ten in the morning. From Ostoi came the most noble chief inspector, Turner—a tall, lean gentleman with maliciously blinking eyes—along with his entire staff of officials. The investigation began.

These gentlemen "from above" already had a preconceived view of the affair. In the opinion of the chief inspector the signals were originating from one of the trackwalker's booths along the Dabrowa–Glaszow line. It only needed to be ascertained which one. According to the official records, there were ten booths in this region; from this number, eight could be eliminated, as they did not possess the apparatus to give signals of this type. Consequently, the suspicion fell on the remaining two. The chief inspector decided to investigate both.

After a lavish dinner at the stationmaster's residence, the inquiry committee set out in a special train at noon. After a half-hour ride, the gentlemen got off before the booth of trackwalker Dziwota; he was one of the suspects.

The poor little fellow, terrified by the invasion of the unexpected visitors, forgot his tongue and answered questions as if awakened from a deep sleep. After an examination that lasted over an hour, the commission decided that Dziwota was as innocent as a lamb and ignorant about everything.

In order not to waste time, the chief inspector left him in peace, recommending to his people a further drive to the eighth trackwalker on the line, on whom his investigation was now focused.

Forty minutes later they stopped at the place. No one ran out to meet them. This made them wonder. The post looked deserted; no trace of life in the homestead, no sign of a living being about. No voice of the man of the house responded, no rooster crowed, no chicken grumbled.

Along steep, little stairs, framed by handrails, they went up the hill on which stood the house of trackwalker Jazwa. At the entrance they were met by countless swarms of flies—nasty, vicious, buzzing. As if angered at the intruders, the insects threw themselves on their hands, eyes, and faces.

The door was knocked on. No one answered from within. One of the railwaymen pressed down on the handle—the door was closed. . . .

"Mr Tuziak," beckoned Pomian to the station locksmith, "pick it."

"With pleasure, stationmaster."

Iron creaked, the lock crunched and yielded.

The inspector pried the door open with his leg and entered. But then he retreated to the open air, applying a handkerchief to his nose. A horrible foulness from inside hit those present. One of the officials ventured to cross the threshold and glanced into the interior.

By a table near the window sat the trackwalker with his head sunk on his chest, the fingers of his right hand resting on the knob of the signal apparatus.

The official advanced towards the table and, paling, turned back to the exit. A quick glance thrown at the trackwalker's hand had ascertained that is was not fingers that were enclosing the knob, but three naked bones, cleansed of meat.

At that moment the sitter by the table wavered and tumbled down like a log onto the ground. Jazwa's body was recognized in a state of complete decomposition. The doctor present ascertained that death came at least ten days earlier.

An official record was written down, and the corpse was buried on the spot, an autopsy being abandoned because of the greatly-advanced deterioration of the body.

The cause of death was not discovered. Peasants from the neighboring village were queried, but could not shed any light on the matter other than that Jazwa had not been seen for a long time. Two hours later the commission returned to Ostoi.

Stationmaster Dabrowa slept calmly that night and the next, undisturbed by signals. But a week later a terrible collision occurred on the Dabrowa–Glaszow line. Cars that had come apart by an unfortunate accident ran into an express train bound for the opposite direction, shattering it completely. The entire train personnel perished, as well as eighty or so travellers.

THE SIDING

In the passenger train heading to Gron at a late autumn hour the crush was enormous; the compartments were packed, the atmosphere was stifling and hot. Due to the lack of space, class differentiations had been obliterated; under an ancient illegal law one sat or stood where one could. Above the chaotic assemblage of heads, lamps were burning with a small, dim light that drifted from car ceilings onto weary faces, rumpled profiles. Tobacco smoke rose in sour fumes and was drawn out in a long, grey line along the corridors to billow in clouds and exit through the abyss of the windows. The steady clatter of wheels acted soporifically, inducing through their monotonous knocking a drowsiness that prevailed in the cars. Chug-chug-chug . . . chug-chug-chug. . . .

Only in one of the third-class compartments, the fifth car before the end, had the ambience not surrendered to the general mood. Here the throng was loud, lively, animated. The attention of the travellers had been entirely captured by a small hunchbacked fellow in a railwayman's uniform of lower ranking who was intently narrating something and underlining his words with colorful and expressive gestures. The clustered-about listeners did not lower their eyes from this person; some, to hear better, got up from other areas of the car and came closer to the centre bench; a curious few had put their heads through the door of the neighboring compartment.

The railwayman was speaking. In the washed-out lamplight that flickered with the tossing of the car, his head moved in an odd cadence, a large, misshapen head with dishevelled grey hair. The wide face, broken erratically on the line of the nose, paled or flushed purply in a rhythm of stormy blood—the exclusive, unique, obstinate face of a fanatic. The eyes glided absentmindedly about those present, glowing with the fire of stubborn thoughts strengthened through the years. And yet this person had moments of beauty. At times it seemed that the hump and the ugliness of the facial features disappeared, and the eyes took on a sapphiric radiance, infused with inspiration, and in the dwarfish figure breathed a noble, irresistible passion. After a moment the metamorphosis weakened, expired, and inside the circle of listeners sat only an entertaining but ugly narrator in a railwayman's shirt.

Professor Ryszpans—a tall, lean man in light-grey attire, a monocle in one eye—had been passing discreetly through the attentive compartment, when he stopped suddenly to glance carefully at the speaker. Something intrigued him, some phrase thrown from the hunchback's lips riveted him in place. He rested an elbow against an iron bar of a partition, tightened in his monocle, and listened.

"Yes, ladies and gentlemen," the railwayman was saying, "in recent times puzzling occurrences have been happening more frequently in the train world. All this seems to have its own purpose, it's clearly heading towards something irrevocable."

He became silent for a moment, blew away the ashes from his pipe, then began talking again:

"Has anyone heard of 'the car of laughter?'"

"Yes, indeed," cut in the professor. "I read something about it a year ago in the newspapers, but superficially, and didn't attach any importance to it; the affair appeared to be journalistic gossip."

"Nothing of the kind, my dear sir!" contested the railwayman passionately, turning to the new listener. "Nice gossip! An obvious truth, a fact ascertained by the testimony of eyewitnesses. I've talked to people who rode in this car. Everyone became ill a week after that ride."

"Please tell us exactly what happened," responded a few voices. "An interesting affair!"

"Not so much interesting, as it is amusing," corrected the dwarf, shaking his lion-like mop. "A year ago some short-lived car briefly wormed its way among its solid and serious companions, and, to people's delight and irritation, it roved on railway lines for upwards of two weeks. Its facetiousness was of a suspicious nature, at times resembling mischievousness. Whoever entered the car, immediately fell into an extremely cheerful mood, which soon developed into explosive hilarity. People would burst out laughing for no apparent reason, as if taking nitrous oxide. They held themselves by the belly, they doubled over, tears streaming down their faces. Finally their laughter took on the threatening characteristic of a paroxysm. In tears of demonic joy, passengers had endless convulsions; as if demented, they threw themselves against walls; and, grunting like a herd of swine, they foamed at the mouth. At various stations, one had to remove several of these unhappy happy persons from the car, for a fear arose that otherwise they would simply burst from laughter."

"How did the railroad authorities respond to this?" asked a stocky man with a strong profile, a designing engineer named Znieslawski, taking advantage of the pause.

"Initially, these gentlemen believed some psychic pestilence was involved that was transferring itself from rider to rider. But when similar occurrences began to repeat themselves, and always in the same car, one railway doctor hit upon a brilliant idea. Assuming that somewhere in the car resided a laughter bacterium, which he hastily named *bacillus ridiculentus* and also *bacillus gelasticus primitivus*, he submitted the infected car to a thorough disinfection."

"Ha, ha, ha!" boomed a professionally interested neighbor, some doctor from W., in the ear of the matchless conversationalist. "I wonder what antiseptic agent he used—Lysol or carbolic acid?"

"You are mistaken, my dear sir; none of those mentioned. The unfortunate car was washed from the roof to the rails with a special preparation devised *ad hoc* by the aforementioned doctor; it was named by its creator *lacrima tristis*, or 'the tear of the sad.'"

"Ha, ha, ha!" choked some lady from a corner. "What a precious man you are! Ha, ha, ha! 'The tear of the sad!'"

"Yes, my dear lady," he continued calmly, "for shortly after the release of the cured car into circulation, several travellers took their own lives with a revolver. These types of experiments revenge themselves," he concluded, shaking his head sadly. "Radicalism in these things is unhealthy."

For a while there was silence.

"A couple of months later," the functionary resumed the tale, "alarming rumors began to spread across the country concerning the appearance of a so-called 'transformation car'—*carrus transformans*, as a certain philologist dubbed it—apparently one of the offerings of the new plague. One day, strange changes were noticed in the outward appearance of several passengers who had made a journey in the same ill-fated car. Families and acquaintances could in no manner recognize the warmly greeting individuals who had exited the train. The female judge K., a young and attractive brunette, repulsed with horror the poxed stranger with a pronounced bald spot who was stubbornly insisting that he was her husband; Miss W., a beautiful eighteen-year-old blonde, went into spasms in the embrace of a grey-haired and podagric old gentleman who had presented himself to her, with a bouquet of azaleas, as her 'fiancé.' On the other hand, the already well-advanced in years lady councillor Z. found herself, with pleasant surprise, at the side of an elegant young man restored miraculously by upwards of forty years, an appellate advisor and her husband.

"At news of this, a huge commotion arose in town. Nothing else was talked about save the puzzling metamorphoses. After a month a new sensation: the bewitched ladies and gentlemen slowly regained their original look, reverting to their time-honored outward appearance."

"And was the car disinfected this time?" asked some woman with interest.

"No, my dear lady, these precautionary measures were waived. On the contrary, the rail authorities surrounded the car with special care when it became apparent that the railroad could derive great profit from it. Special tickets were even printed up to gain entrance to this wonderful car, so-called 'transformation tickets.' The demand was naturally huge. At the front of the queue were long columns of old ladies, ugly widows, and spinsters insisting on the travel tickets. The candidates voluntarily inflated the cost; they paid three to four times in excess of the price; they bribed clerks, conductors, even porters. In the car, before the car, and under the car dramatic scenes were played out, sometimes passing over into bloody fights. Several grey-haired women expired in one skirmish. This horrible example did not, however, cool down the lust for rejuvenation: the massacre continued. Finally, the entire disturbance was put to an end by the wonderful car itself. After two weeks of transformation activity, it suddenly lost its strange power. Stations took on a normal appearance; the cadres of old men and women retreated back to their firesides and cozy sleeping nooks."

The hunchback stopped talking, and in the midst of the din of stirred voices, laughter, and jokes on the subject presented by the story, he slipped furtively from the car.

Ryszpans followed him like a shadow. He was intrigued by this railwayman with the darned-at-the-elbow shirt who had expressed himself more properly than many an average intellectual. Something drew him to the man, some mysterious current of sympathy impelled him towards the eccentric invalid.

In the corridor of first-class compartments, he laid a hand lightly on his shoulder.

"Excuse me. Can I have a few words with you?"

The hunchback smiled with satisfaction.

"Certainly. I'll even show you to a place where we'll be able to talk freely. I know this car inside out."

And pulling the professor after him, he turned left, where the compartments broke off into a thin corridor leading to the platform. Unusually, no one was here. The railwayman showed his companion the wall enclosing the last car.

"Do you see that small ledge at the top? It's a concealed lock. It's hidden for the use of railway dignitaries in exceptional cases. In a moment, we'll see it more clearly."

He moved aside the ledge, took out from his pocket a conductor's key and, putting it in the opening, turned it. At that moment, a steel blind smoothly rolled up, revealing a small, elegantly furnished compartment.

"Please enter," urged the railwayman.

Soon they were sitting on soft, upholstered cushions, sealed off from the din and throngs by the lowered blind.

The functionary looked at the professor with an expression of anticipation. Ryszpans did not hurry with a question. He frowned, set in his monocle tighter, and sank into thought. After a moment, not looking at his companion, he began:

"I was struck by the contrast between the humorous occurrences you had related and the serious elucidation which preceded them. If I remember correctly, you said that puzzling events have been occurring in recent times which are heading towards some goal. If I understood the tone of your words well, you were speaking seriously; one had the impression that you consider this goal as grave, maybe even decisive...."

A mysterious smile brightened up the hunchback's face:

"And you were not mistaken, sir. The contrast will disappear if we'll understand these 'amusing' manifestations as a mocking summons, a provocation, and a prelude to other manifestations, deeper ones, like tests of strength before the release of an unknown energy."

"All right!" exclaimed the professor. "*Du sublime au ridicule il n'y a qu'un pas.* I suspected something of the sort. Otherwise I wouldn't have initiated this discussion."

"You belong, sir, to a rare few. So far I've found only seven individuals on this train who have comprehended these affairs in depth, and who have declared themselves ready to venture with me into the labyrinth of consequences. Maybe I'll find in you an eighth volunteer?"

"That will depend on the depth and quality of the explanations that you owe me."

"Certainly. That is why I'm here. To begin with, you should know that these mysterious cars came onto the line straight from a siding."

"What does that mean?"

"It means that before they were let out into circulation, they rested for a long time on a siding and breathed in its atmosphere."

"I don't understand. In the first place, what is a siding?"

"A spurned offshoot of rail, a solitary branch of track stretching out from 50 to 100 meters, without exit, without an outlet; closed off by an artificial hill and a barrier; like a withered branch of a green tree, like the stump of a mutilated hand...."

A deep, tragic lyricism flowed from the railwayman's words. The professor looked at him in amazement, as he went on:

"Neglect is all about: weeds overgrowing rusty rails; wanton field grass, oraches, wild chamomile plants, and thistles. Over to the side the plates of a decrepit switch are falling off; the glass of the lantern is broken, a lantern that doesn't have anyone to light the way for at night. And why should it? After all, the track is closed; you wouldn't be able to go up more than a hundred meters. Not too far away the engine traffic is vibrant with activity, the railway's arteries pulsate with life. Here it is eternally quiet. Sometimes a switching engine loses its way onto the track, sometimes an unattached coach reluctantly crowds in; now and then a freight car worn out by riding will enter for a longer rest, reeling heavily, lazily, to stand in silence for entire months or years. On a decaying roof a bird will build a nest and feed its young, in the cracks of a platform weeds will proliferate, a wicker branch will burst forth. Above the rusted rails, a broken-down semaphore dips its dislocated arms and blesses the melancholic ruins. . . ."

The voice of the railwayman broke. The professor sensed his emotion; the lyricism of the description astounded and thrilled him at the same time. But from whence came that touch of mournfulness?

After a while, the professor said, "I felt the poetry of the siding, but I'm unable to explain to myself how its atmosphere could cause the aforementioned manifestations."

"From this poetry," enlightened the hunchback, "flows a deep theme of yearning—a yearning towards unending distances whose access is closed off by a landmark, a nailed-up wooden barrier. There, beside it, trains speed by, engines hurry away into the wide, beautiful world; here, the dull border of a grassy hill. A yearning of the handicapped. Do you understand, sir? A yearning without a hope of realization creates contempt and feeds upon itself, until it overgrows through the strength of its desires the fortunate reality of—privilege. Hidden energies are born, forces accumulate for years. Who knows if they will not explode with the elements? And then they will transcend commonplaceness to fulfill higher tasks more beautiful than reality. They reach beyond it. . . ."

"And where can one find that siding? I assume that you have a particular place in mind?"

"Hmm, that depends," he said, smiling. "For certain there was a point of exit. But there are many sidings everywhere, by every station. It could be this one, it could be that one."

"Yes, yes, but I'm talking about the one from which those cars came."

The hunchback shook his head impatiently:

"We do not understand one another. Who knows—maybe that mysterious siding can be found everywhere? One only has to know how to seek it out, track it down—one has to know how to run into it, drive up to it, to enter into its grove. So far, only one person has succeeded in this. . . ."

He stopped and gazed deeply at the professor with eyes opalescent with violet light.

"Who?" asked the other mechanically.

"Trackwalker Wior. Wior, the hunchbacked, cruelly handicapped by nature trackwalker, is today the king of the sidings and their sad spirit yearning for release."

"I understand," murmured Ryszpans.

"Trackwalker Wior," finished the railwayman passionately, "formerly a scholar, thinker, philosopher—thrown by the vagaries of fate among the rails of scorned track—a voluntary watchman over forgotten lines—a fanatic among people. . . ."

They rose and made their way towards the exit. Ryszpans gave him his hand.

"Agreed," he said strongly.

The steel blind went up, and they entered the corridor.

"Till we meet again," the hunchback bid his farewell. "I'm going to catch some more souls. Three cars remain. . . ."

And he disappeared through the door connecting to the adjacent coach.

Lost in thought, the professor went over to a window, cut a cigar, and lit it.

Darkness reigned outside. Lamplights peering out into space from quadrangle windows moved quickly along the slopes in a fleeting reconnaissance: the train was proceeding alongside some empty meadows and pastures. . . .

A man came up to the professor, requesting a light. Ryszpans blew out the ashes from his cigar and politely handed the cigar to the stranger.

"Thank you." The engineer introduced himself: "Znieslawski."

A conversation was struck up.

"Have you noticed how empty it has suddenly become?" Znieslawski asked, casting an eye about. "The corridor is completely deserted. I glanced into two compartments to discover pleasurably that both had plenty of room."

"I wonder what it's like in the other classes," replied Ryszpans.

"We can take a look!"

And heading towards the end of the train, they passed through several cars. Everywhere they noticed a substantial decrease in the number of travellers.

"Strange," said the professor. "Less than half an hour ago the crush was still terrible; within that short period the train has just stopped once."

"That's right," confirmed Znieslawski. "Apparently many people must have left the train at that time. I don't understand how such a discharge of passengers could occur at one station—and an insignificant one, at that."

They sat down on one of the benches in a second-class compartment. By the window two men were talking in an undertone. Ryszpans and Znieslawski caught a part of their conversation:

"You know," a bureaucratic-looking passenger was saying, "something is telling me to get off this train."

"That's odd!" answered the other. "It's the same with me. A stupid feeling. I must be in Zaszum today and must go this way— nevertheless, I will get off at the next station and wait for the morning train. What a waste of time!"

"I'll do likewise, though it is also inconvenient for me. I'll be late for work by several hours. But I can't do anything else. I won't go farther on this train."

"Excuse me," Znieslawski cut in, "what exactly impels both of you gentlemen to make such an inconvenient departure from this train?"

"I don't know," answered the official. "Some type of vague feeling."

"A sort of internal command," explained his companion.

"Maybe an oppressive, unknown fear," suggested Ryszpans, winking his eye a little maliciously.

"Maybe," countered the passenger calmly. "But I'm not ashamed of it. The feeling which I'm now experiencing is so special, so *sui generis*, that it can't be defined by what we generally call fear."

Znieslawski glanced knowingly at the professor.

"Maybe we should go farther up?"

After a while, they found themselves in a nearly deserted third-class compartment. Here, in the fumes of cigar smoke, sat three men and two women. One of the latter, a comely townswoman, was talking to her companion:

"That Zietulska is strange! She was going to Zupnik with me, and meanwhile she gets off halfway, four miles before her destination."

"She didn't say why?' questioned the second woman.

"She did, but I don't believe her. She supposedly grew faint and couldn't ride the train farther. God knows what the truth is."

"What about those fellows who were so loudly promising themselves a good time at Gron tomorrow morning—didn't they get off at Pytom? They became quieter after we left Turon and began pacing about the car—and then it was suddenly as if someone had swept them out of the compartment. You know, even I feel strange here...."

In the next car both men became sensitized to a mood of nervousness and anxiety. People were rapidly taking down their luggage from overhanging nets, impatiently looking through windows, pressing against one another towards the platform exit.

"What the devil?" muttered Ryszpans. "A thoroughly distinguished group—all elegant ladies and gentlemen. Why do these people want to get off at the nearest station? If I remember, it is some out-of-the-way little place."

"Indeed," admitted the engineer. "It is Drohiczyn, a stop in the middle of a field, a God-forsaken hole. Apparently there's only the station, a post office, and a police station. Hmm . . . interesting! What are they going to do there in the middle of the night?"

He glanced at his watch.

"It's only two."

The professor shook his head. "I'm reminded of some interesting conclusions a certain psychologist reached after thoroughly studying fatality statistics in railway accidents."

"What kind of conclusions?"

"He claimed the losses were not as great as one would suppose. The statistics showed that trains that met with an accident were always less occupied than others. Apparently people got off in time or else they completely refrained from a ride on the deadly trains; others were stopped right before their trip by some unexpected obstacle; a portion were suddenly seized with ill-health or some longer sickness."

"I understand," said Znieslawski. "Everything depended on the increase in the instinct of self-preservation, which, according to the tension, assumed various hues; in some persons it was emphasized strongly, in others, weakly. So, you believe that what we see and hear now can be explained in a similar manner?"

"I don't know. This association just occurred to me. Yet even if it were true, I'm glad an opportunity has arisen to observe this phenomenon. I actually should have got off at a previous station that was my destination. As you see, I'm going farther of my own free will."

"Splendid!" remarked the engineer with approval. "I also will maintain my post—though, I admit, I've had a peculiar feeling for a certain time, something like an unease or a tense anticipation. Are you really free from these?"

"Well...no," the professor said slowly. "You are right. Something's in the air; we are not completely normal here. In me, however, the result manifests itself in an interest as to what's ahead, what will evolve out of this."

"In that case we both stand on the same platform. I even believe that we have several companions. Wior's influence, as I see, has encompassed certain circles."

The professor gave a start.

"So you know this man?"

"Naturally. I sensed in you his follower. Here's to 'The Siding Brotherhood!'"

The engineer's cry was interrupted by the grind of braking wheels: the train had stopped before the station. Multitudes of travellers poured out through open car doors. In the station's pale lamplights one could see the faces of the railway official and the sole switchman for the entire way-station observing in amazement the unusual influx of guests for Drohiczyn.

"Stationmaster, will we find sleeping accommodations here for the night?" some elegant gentleman in a cylinder hat asked humbly.

"Maybe on a block on the floor, most-esteemed sir," the switchman offered in answer.

"It's going to be difficult getting some lodging, my dear Madame," the stationmaster explained to some ermined lady. "It's two hours to the nearest village."

"Jesus Mary! We've fallen into it!" lamented a thin feminine voice from the throng.

"All aboard!" called out the impatient official.

"All aboard, all aboard!" repeated two uncertain voices in the darkness.

The train moved. At the moment when the station was slipping into the obscurity of the night, Znieslawski, leaning out from a window, pointed to a group of people at the side of the station's platform.

"Do you see those persons to the left of that wall?"

"Why, yes. They're the conductors of our train."

"Ha, ha, ha! *Periculum in mora*, professor! The rats are deserting the ship. A bad sign!"

"Ha, ha, ha!" joined in the professor. "A train without conductors! All hell's broken loose!"

"No, no, it's not that bad," pacified Znieslawski. "Two have remained. Look there—one has just closed the compartment; the other one I saw jumping on the running board at the moment of departure."

"The followers of Wior," explained Ryszpans. "It would be worthwhile finding out how many people have remained on this train."

They went through several cars. In one, they came across an aesthetic-faced monk deep in prayer; in another, two clean-shaven men bearing the look of actors; a few cars were completely empty. In the corridor running lengthwise through a second-class compartment, several persons with luggage in hand were milling about, their eyes uneasy, their nervous movements betraying agitation.

"For sure they wanted to get off at Drohiczyn, but at the last moment they changed their minds," Znieslawski threw out the assumption.

"And now they regret it," added Ryszpans.

At that moment the hunchbacked railwayman showed up at the platform of the car. A sinister, demonic smile was playing over his face. Behind him was a drawn-out file of several travellers. Coming to the professor and his companion, Wior greeted them as if he were a familiar acquaintance:

"The revue is over. Please follow me."

A woman's cry reverberated at the end of the corridor. The men glanced to that side and caught sight of a passenger's body disappearing through an open door.

"Did that person fall or jump?" asked a few voices.

As if in answer, a second passenger plunged into the abyss of space; after him hurried a third; then the rest of the nervous group threw themselves in wild flight.

"Have they gone crazy?" someone asked from inside. "Jumping out of a train at full speed? Well, well. . . ."

"They were in a hurry to know Mother Earth," said Znieslawski casually.

Not attributing greater importance to the incident, they returned to the compartment into which had disappeared the trackwalker. Here, aside from Wior, they found ten people, among them two conductors and three women. Everyone sat down on a bench and gazed attentively at the hunchbacked railwayman, who had gone to stand in the centre of the compartment.

"Ladies and gentlemen," he began, taking in those present with the fire of his glance. "All of us, including me, comprise thirteen individuals. A fatal number! No . . . I'm mistaken—fourteen including my engine driver, and he is also my man. A mere handful, a handful, but it is enough for me. . . ."

These last words he finished saying half-aloud, as if to himself, and he became momentarily silent. One could only hear the clatter of the rails and the rumble of the car's wheels.

"Ladies and gentlemen," resumed Wior. "A special moment has arrived, a moment when the yearning of many years will be realized. This train already belongs to us. We jointly took possession of it; foreign, indifferent, and hostile elements have been eliminated from its organism. Here rules the absolute atmosphere and power of the siding. In a moment that power will manifest itself. Whoever does not feel sufficiently ready should withdraw now; later, it may be too late. Space. The space is free and the door is open. I guarantee safety. So?" He threw a searching glance about. "So no one is withdrawing?"

In answer came a deep silence vibrant with the quickened breathing of twelve human chests.

Wior smiled triumphantly.

"Good. Everyone remains here of their own free will, everyone is responsible for their own decision at this moment."

The travellers were silent. Their restless eyes, smouldering with feverish light, did not leave the trackwalker's face. One of the women suddenly got an attack of hysterical laughter, which under the steady, cold glance of Wior quickly passed. The railwayman drew out from his breast pocket a quadrangle paper with some drawing on it.

"Here is the road we have so far been travelling on," he said, pointing to a double line that blackened the paper. "Here, on the right, this small point—that's Drohiczyn, which we passed a moment ago. This other point, the large one at the top, is Gron, the last station on this line. But we will not reach it—that destination is of no concern to us now."

He paused and stared intently at the drawing. A shudder of terror shook his listeners. Wior's words fell heavily on the spirit like molten lead.

"And here, to the left," he further explained, moving a pointed finger, "appears a crimson line. Do you see its red trail winding ever farther away from the main track? That's the siding line. We are supposed to enter onto it."

He became quiet again and studied the bloody ribbon.

From outside came the clangor of unleashed wheels. The train had apparently doubled its velocity and was speeding along in maniacal fury.

The trackwalker spoke:

"The time has come. Let everyone assume a sitting or lying position. Yes . . . good," he finished up, passing a careful glance over the travellers, who had fulfilled his instructions as if hypnotized. "Now I can begin. Attention! In a minute we'll be turning onto the siding. . . ."

Holding the drawing in his right hand at eye level, he fixed his eyes on it one more time with the fanatical glare of his suddenly widened pupils. Then he stiffened like a board, letting the paper drop from his hand, and stood frozen in the middle of the compartment; his eyes rolled up so strongly that one could only see the edges of the whites; his face assumed a stony expression. Suddenly he started to walk stiffly to the open window. He propped himself against the lower frame and bounced off the floor with his legs, leaning out half of his body into space; his figure, stretched out beyond the window like a magnetic needle, wavered a few times on the edge of the frame, then placed itself at an angle to the wall of the car. . . .

Suddenly a hellish bang resounded, as of cars smashing, a ferocious crash of crushed scrap-iron, a din of rails, buffers, a rattling of riotous wheels and chains. In the midst of the tumult of benches splitting into fragments, doors tumbling down, in the midst of the rumble of collapsing ceilings, floors, walls, in the midst of the clashing of bursting pipes, tubes, tanks, the locomotive's whistle groaned in despair. . . .

Suddenly everything receded, was driven into the ground, was blown away, and the ears were filled with a great, powerful, boundless noise.

And this noisy duration enveloped the world for a long, long time, and it seemed that every earthly waterfall was playing a song of menace and that all earthly trees were rustling scores of leaves. Afterwards, even this died down, and the great silence of darkness spread over the world. In the still and silent heavens, someone's invisible, someone's very caressing hands stretched out and stroked the palls of space soothingly. And under this gentle caress, soft waves were tossed about, flowing in by quiet pipes and rocking one to sleep . . . to sweet, silent sleep. . . .

At some moment the professor woke up. He glanced half-consciously at the surroundings and noticed that he was in an empty compartment. A vague feeling of strangeness seized him; everything beyond him appeared somehow different, somehow new, something one had to get used to. But the adjustment was oddly difficult and slow. In effect, one completely had to change one's point of view and the way one looked at things. Ryszpans gave the impression of a person who enters into the light of day after a lengthy wandering in a mile-long tunnel. He looked with eyes blinded by darkness, he rubbed away the mist covering his sight. He started to remember. . . .

In his mind faded recollections followed each other, recollections that had preceded . . . this. Some type of crash, din, some type of sudden impact that had levelled all sensations and consciousness. . . .

An accident!—his haziness told him indistinctly.

He glanced carefully at himself, ran his hand about his face, his forehead—nothing! Not even a drop of blood, no pain.

"*Cogito—ergo—sum*! " he pronounced finally.

A desire arose within him to walk about the compartment. He left his place, raised his leg and—was suspended a couple of inches off the floor.

"What the hell!" he muttered in astonishment. "Have I lost my proper weight or what? I feel light as a feather."

And he drifted up, until he reached the ceiling of the car.

"But what happened to the others?" he asked himself, going down to the door of the neighboring compartment.

At that moment he discovered Znieslawski at the entrance, who, likewise raised a couple of centimeters above the floor, shook his hand warmly.

"Greetings! I see you're also not in complete accordance with the laws of gravity?"

"Ha, what can one do?" Ryszpans sighed out in resignation. "You're not injured?"

"God forbid!" assured the engineer. "I'm in the best of health. I awoke just a moment ago."

"A peculiar awakening. I wonder where we are exactly?"

"So do I. It seems we're tearing along at a terrific speed."

They looked out the window. Nothing. Emptiness. Only a strong, cool current blowing outside gave the impression that the train was running furiously along.

"That's strange," remarked Ryszpans. "I absolutely don't see a thing. Emptiness above, emptiness before me."

"How extraordinary! It's supposedly daytime, because it's bright, but one can't see the sun, and there's no fog. We're moving as if in space—what time could it be?"

They both glanced at their watches. After a moment, Znieslawski raised his eyes to his companion and met a glance that said the same thing.

"I can't make anything out. The hours have merged into a black, wavy line...."

"And the hands are wandering around, not telling anything."

"The waves of duration flowing one to the other, without beginning or end..."

"The twilight of time...."

"Look," Znieslawski suddenly called out, pointing to the opposite side of the car. "I see someone from our group through the wall, that monk—remember him?"

"Yes. That's the Carmelite, Brother Jozef. I've talked with him. He's already spotted us—he's smiling and giving us signs. What paradoxical effects. We're looking through that wall as if through glass!"

"Our bodies' opaqueness has completely gone to hell," the engineer concluded.

"It's no better, it seems, with our impermeableness," answered Ryszpans, passing through the wall to the other compartment.

"Indeed," admitted Znieslawski, following his example. And they went through the wall and several others, until in the third car they greeted Brother Jozef.

The Carmelite had just finished his morning prayer, and, restrengthened, was sincerely pleased with the meeting.

"Great works of the Lord!" he said, raising distant eyes clouded over with the mist of meditation. "We are living through strange moments. We've all been wonderfully awakened. Glory to the Everlasting One! Let's go and connect up with the rest of our brothers."

"We are with you," echoed back several voices from all sides, and through the walls of the car ten figures passed and surrounded the talkers. These people were of various occupations and professions, including the engine driver of the train and three women. Everyone's eyes were involuntarily looking for someone; everyone instinctively felt the absence of one companion.

"There are thirteen of us," said a lean, sharp-faced young man. "I do not see Master Wior."

"Master Wior will not come," said Brother Jozef, as if in a dream. "Do not look for trackwalker Wior here. Look deeper, my brothers, look into your souls. Maybe you'll find him."

They ceased talking, and they understood. Across their faces flowed a great peace, and they glowed with a strange light. And they read their own souls and fathomed one another in a wonderful clairvoyance.

"Brothers!' resumed the monk, "our bodies are given to us for only a little time longer; in a few moments we may have to abandon them. Then we will part company. Everyone will go their own direction, carried by their own destiny that was forged in the book of fate ages ago; everyone will make their way on their own path, to their own area, which was preordained on the other side. Multitudes of our brothers' souls await us with yearning. Before the moment of parting arrives, listen once more to a voice from the other side. The words that I'll read to you were written ten days ago, measuring time in an earthly manner."

Finishing this, he unfolded some newspaper sheets, barely rustling them, and began to read in a deep, penetrating voice:

"NW., November 15, 1950. Mysterious Disaster. A mysterious, unexplained event occurred yesterday, the night of the 14th–15th, on the Zalesna–Gron railway line. It concerns the fate that met passenger train number 20 between the hours of two to three after midnight. The actual disaster was preceded by strange fears. As if having a presentiment of ominous danger, passengers had been getting off in droves at stations and stops before the place of the fatal accident, even though their destination was considerably farther. Asked by station officials about the reason for cutting short their journey, these people were vague in their explanations, as if not wanting to reveal their motives for this odd behavior. More characteristic is the fact that at Drohiczyn several on-duty conductors deserted the train, preferring to risk severe punishment and the loss of their jobs rather than riding farther; only three persons from the entire train personnel remained at their posts. The train left Drohiczyn nearly empty. Several undecided travellers, who at the last minute had drawn back inside the cars, jumped out fifteen minutes later while the train was in motion through an open field. By some miracle these people came away uninjured, returning to Drohiczyn on foot around four in the morning. They were witnesses to the last moments of the ill-fated train before the disaster, which had to have occurred several minutes later.

"Around five in the morning, the first alarm signal came from the booth of trackwalker Zola, situated five kilometers beyond Drohiczyn. The manager of the station got on a trolley and in half an hour stood at the place of the accident, where he met an investigating committee from Rakwa.

"An odd picture greeted those present. In an open field several hundred meters beyond the trackwalker's booth, a severed train stood on the tracks. The two rear cars were completely untouched, then came a break corresponding to the length of three cars; and again two cars in a normal state connected by chains—a one car gap—and finally a tender at the front, its locomotive missing. There were no traces of blood on the tracks, the platforms, or the steps, nowhere were there any wounded or killed. Inside the cars it was also empty and quiet; not one compartment contained a corpse, and not the slightest damage was discovered in those cars present.

"The visual particulars were written down and sent to headquarters. The railway authorities do not expect a speedy clearing up of this mystery."

The Carmelite became silent for a moment, put aside the paper, and then started to read from a second one:

"W., November 25, 1950. Amazing revelations and details concerning the train disaster of the 15th of this month. The mysterious events, which were played out on the railway line beyond Drohiczyn the 15th of this month, have not been explained to the present time. On the contrary, ever-deeper shadows fall on the incident and cloud any understanding of it.

"This day brought a series of astounding bits of information in connection with the accident that darken the affair even more and give rise to serious, far reaching reflections. Here is a summary of what telegrams from authentic sources tell us:

"Today at daybreak, the 25th of this month, those cars of passenger train number 20, whose absence was noted ten days ago, showed up on the exact spot of the disaster. Significantly, the cars turned up on that space not as one solid train, but disunited in groups of one, two, or three, corresponding to the gaps noticed visually on the 15th of this month. Before the first car, at the distance of a tender, the locomotive turned up completely intact.

"Terrified at this sudden appearance, railwaymen at first did not dare to approach the cars, considering them phantoms or a result of hallucinations. Finally, though, when the cars did not vanish, they plucked up enough courage to enter within.

"Here their eyes were presented with a terrible sight. In one of the compartments they found the bodies of thirteen individuals stretched out on benches or in sitting positions. The cause of death is so far undetermined. The bodies of these unfortunates do not exhibit any external or internal injuries; also there are no traces of asphyxiation or poisoning. The deaths of the casualties will apparently remain an unsolvable puzzle.

"Among the thirteen individuals who met with a mysterious demise, the identity of six has so far been ascertained: Brother Jozef Zygwulski, from the Carmelite order and an author of several deeply mystical tracts; Prof. Ryszpans, an illustrious psychologist; Engineer Znieslawski, a respected inventor; Stwosz, the engine driver of the train; and two conductors. The names of the other persons are thus far unknown.

"News of this mysterious event flew like lightning throughout the entire country, bringing forth startling impressions everywhere. Already numerous, sometimes profound, interpretations and commentaries have appeared in newspapers. Voices are heard, branding the defined 'railroad disaster' occurrences as false and ridiculous.

"The Society of Psychic Research is apparently already planning a series of lectures, which several distinguished psychologists and psychiatrists will deliver in the upcoming days.

"This matter will probably drag on for many years in the sciences, revealing new and unknown horizons."

Brother Jozef finished, and in an already fading voice he addressed his companions:

"Brothers! The moment of parting has arrived. Our bodies are already separating."

"We've crossed the border between life and death," the professor's voice resounded like a distant echo.

"To enter into a reality of a higher order...."

The walls of the cars, misty like clouds, started to part, dissolve, deteriorate.... Indistinct sheets of roofs were sawn off, ethereal coils of platforms were deflected forever into space, together with gaseous spirals of pipes, tubes, buffers....

The figures of the travellers, limp and completely transparent, weakened, disintegrated, came apart in pieces....

"Farewell, brothers, farewell!..."

Voices faded, died out, were dispersed... until they became silent somewhere in the interplanetary distances of the beyond....

ULTIMA THULE

It happened ten years ago. The event has already taken on dispersed, almost dreamy forms, covered by the azure mist of things past. Today it seems like a vision or a mad reverie; yet I know that every detail, even the most minor, occurred exactly as I remember it. Since that time many events have passed before my eyes; I have experienced many things, and more than one blow has fallen upon my grey head, but the memory of that incident has remained unchanged, the picture of that strange moment is permanently and deeply etched into my soul; the patina of time has not dimmed its strong outline—on the contrary, it seems that the passage of the years has mysteriously brought its shadows into relief. . . .

At the time I was the stationmaster of Krepacz, a small mountain station not far from the border. From my platform one could see the extended jagged mountain chain of the boundary as clearly as the palm of one's hand.

Krepacz was the next to the last stop on the line heading to the frontier; beyond it, fifty kilometers away, was Szczytnisk, the final station in the country, which was watched over with the vigilance of a borderland crane by Kazimierz Joszt, my fellow colleague and friend.

He liked to compare himself to Charon, and the station charged to his care he renamed, in ancient style, Ultima Thule. This fancy was not just a remnant from his classical studies, as the appropriateness of both names lay deeper than outwardly apparent.

The Szczytnisk region was truly beautiful. Even though it was only a forty-five minute drive by passenger train from my place, it betrayed a fundamentally separate and individual character not met with anywhere in these parts.

Nestling against a huge granite wall that fell straight down, the small station building reminded one of a swallow's nest attached to the recess of a rock. The encompassing peaks, two thousand meters in elevation, plunged the surrounding wide areas, the station, and its warehouses into semi-darkness. The gloom blowing from the tops of these colossi covered the railroad haven with an elusive shroud. Perpetual mists whirled about the peaks and rolled down in wet, turban-like clouds. At the level of a thousand meters, more or less at the middle of its height, the wall formed a ledge in the shape of a huge platform, which, as if magically gouged, was filled to the brim with a silvery deep-blue lake. Several underground streams, fraternizing secretly in the bowels of the mountain, gushed from its side in rainbow-colored waterfalls.

To the left were ranges eternally draped with a green cloak of firs and stone pines; to the right was a wild precipice of dwarf mountain pines; opposite, as if a boundary marker, was the unyielding edge of strong winds. Above was a sky cloudy or reddened by the dawn of a morning sun. And beyond—another world, strange, unknown. A wild, sealed-off spot, ominous with the poetry of peaks forming a boundary.

The station was connected to the rest of the area by a long tunnel forged into the ranges; if not for this tunnel, the isolation of this recess would have been complete.

The rail traffic, wandering among the lonely peaks, dwindled, slackened, spent itself out. A small number of trains, like meteors thrown out of an orbit, emerged infrequently from the depths of the tunnel, and drove up to the platform softly, silently, as if fearful of disturbing the reveries of the mountain giants about.

A train, after unloading its cars, would glide a few meters beyond the platform and into a vaulted hall hewn out of the granite wall. Here it stood for many hours, looking out from the sockets of empty windows to the dim cavern and waiting for a replacement. When the longed-for comrade arrived, the train lazily left the rocky shelter and went out into the world of life, into the fervor of a strongly throbbing pulse. Then the next train would take its place. And again the station would fall into a dreamy slumber wrapped in a veil of mists. The quiet of this secluded spot was interrupted only by a chirrup of eaglets in the surrounding gullies or the noise of rocks tumbling in the ravines.

I loved this mountain hermitage immensely. It was for me a symbol of mysterious lands, a mystical frontier between two worlds, a sort of suspension between Life and Death.

At every available moment, entrusting the care of Krepacz to my assistant, I took a trolley to Szczytnisk to visit my friend Joszt. Our friendship was long-standing; it had been struck up when we were schoolmates and had been strengthened by the bond of our profession and our close proximity to each other.

Joszt never repaid my visits.

"I will not set one foot out of this place," he would typically answer my rebukes. "I will remain here to the end." Taking in the surroundings with an enraptured glance, he would add after a while, "For is it not beautiful here?"

I would silently acknowledge this, and everything continued on as it had before.

My friend Joszt was an unusual person, in every respect strange. Despite his truly dove-like gentleness and unparalleled kindness, he was not well liked in this area. Mountaineers seemed to avoid the stationmaster, getting out of his way from a distance. The reason lay in an odd belief of unknown origin. Joszt had the reputation among the country-folk as a "seer," and this in the negative connotation of the word. It was said that he could foresee in his fellow creatures the "character of death," that he had, as it were, a presentiment of its cold breath on the face of those chosen to die.

How much truth there was in this, I do not know, but, in any event, I noticed in him something that could have upset a suggestible and superstitious mind. The following strange coincidence made a particular impression upon me.

There was at the Szczytnisk station, among other employees, a switchman named Glodzik, a diligent and conscientious worker. Joszt liked him a good deal and treated him not as an inferior but as a friend and fellow professional.

One Sunday, arriving for a visit as usual, I found Joszt in a gloomy mood, sullen and forlorn. When I asked what was the matter, he put me off and maintained his sombre expression. Just then Glodzik showed up to make a report and requested instructions. The stationmaster muttered something, cast a strange glance at the other's eyes, and clasped his coarse, toil-worn hands.

Amazed at the behavior of his superior, the switchman departed, shaking his large curly head incredulously.

"Poor man!" whispered Joszt, looking sadly after him.

"Why?" I asked, not understanding the scene.

Then Joszt explained.

"I had a bad dream last night," he said, avoiding my glance. "A very bad dream."

"Do you believe in dreams?"

"Unfortunately, the one I dreamed is typical and has never proven itself wrong. Last night I saw a secluded old ruin with broken windows. Every time this accursed building appears in my dreams some misfortune occurs."

"What does this house have to do with the switchman?"

"In one of its empty windows I clearly saw his face. He leaned out of this black den and waved towards me a checkered kerchief that he always wears around his neck."

"And so?"

"It was a farewell gesture. That man will die soon—today, tomorrow, at any moment."

"A nightmare's nod, then trust in God," I said, trying to calm him. Joszt merely forced a smile and became silent.

And yet, that day, Glodzik perished through his own mistake. An engine, led astray by a wrong signal he set, cut off both his legs; he died on the spot.

The incident affected me deeply, and for a long time I avoided a conversation with Joszt on the subject. Finally, perhaps a year later, I addressed it in a casual way.

"Since when have you had these ominous premonitions? As far as I remember you never used to exhibit similar abilities."

"You're right," he retorted, disagreeably touching upon the subject. "That cursed ability developed in me only later."

"Forgive me for annoying you with this unpleasant matter, but I'd like to find a way of freeing you from this fatal faculty. When did you first notice it?"

"Eight years ago, more or less."

"Therefore a year after you moved to this area?"

"Yes, a year after coming to Szczytnisk. Then, in December, right on Christmas Eve, I had a presentiment of Groceli's death, who was the chief officer here at the time. The affair became widely known, and in a matter of several days I had secured the sinister nickname 'The Seer'! Mountaineers began to run away from me as from a tawny owl."

"Odd! And yet there must be something to it. What's happening here is a classic example of so-called 'second sight.' A long time ago I read a lot on this subject in books of old magic. Supposedly Scottish and Irish Mountain Men are frequently endowed with a similar ability."

"Yes, I also studied the histories of this manifestation with an obvious interest. It even seems to me that I've found a cause in its general characteristics. Your reference to Scottish Mountain Men is quite apt, only it necessitates a few additional words. You forgot to mention that these people, detested by their neighbors and often driven out like lepers beyond the village limits, exhibit their fatal ability only as long as they stay on the island; when they move to the Continent they lose their sad gift and are no different than the average person."

"Interesting. This would then affirm that this outstanding psychic phenomenon is, after all, dependent on factors of a chthonic nature."

"Indeed. This phenomenon has many telluric elements to it. We are sons of the Earth and are subject to its powerful influences, even in areas ostensibly separated from its core."

"Do you think your own clairvoyance arises from the same source?" I asked after a momentary hesitation.

"Of course. These surroundings influence me; I remain at the mercy of the atmosphere here. My ominous ability has obviously resulted from the spirit of this region. I live on the frontier of two worlds."

"Ultima Thule?" I whispered, bowing my head.

"Ultima Thule!" Joszt repeated like an echo.

Gripped by fear, I ceased talking. After a while, shaking off this feeling, I asked: "Since you clearly understand everything, why haven't you moved to another place?"

"I can't. I absolutely can't. I feel that if I left, I should act against my destiny."

"You're superstitious, Kazik."

"No, this is not superstition. This is destiny. I have a deep belief that only here, on this patch of earth, will I fulfill some important mission. What it is, I don't know exactly; I only have a slight inkling of it."

He broke off, as if frightened by what he had said. After a moment, turning his grey eyes to the rocky wall of the border, eyes shining from the glare of the sunset, he added in a low voice:

"Do you know that it sometimes seems to me that here at this perpendicular boundary the visible world ends and that there, on the other side, begins a different, new world, a *mare tenebrarum* unknown in the human language."

He lowered his eyes, wearied from the summits' crimson glow, towards the ground, and then turned to the opposite direction where lay the train area.

"And here," he added, "here life ends. Here is its final exertion, its last outskirt. Here its creative force is depleted. And so I stand in this place as a sentry over Life and Death, as a trustee of the secrets on this and the other side of the grave."

Saying these words, he looked deeply into my face. He was beautiful at that moment. The infused, inspired glance of meditative eyes, the eyes of a poet and a mystic, had so much fire concentrated in them that I could not bear their radiant power, and I bent my head in reverence. Then he asked a final question:

"Do you believe in life after death?"

I raised my head slowly. "I know nothing. People say there are as many proofs for as against. I'd like to believe in it."

"The dead live," Joszt said firmly.

Then came a long intense silence.

Meanwhile the sun, after outlining an arch over the toothy ravine, concealed its disc behind the horizon.

"It's late already," observed Joszt, "and shadows are descending from the mountains. You have to rest early today; the journey has tired you."

Thus ended our memorable conversation. From then on we did not talk about death or the menacing gift of second sight. I steered clear of discussions on this dangerous latter subject, for it apparently caused him pain.

Until one day he himself reminded me of his gloomy abilities.

That was ten years ago, in the middle of summer, in July. The dates of these events I remember clearly; they are forever imprinted in my mind.

It was Wednesday, the 13th of July, a holiday. As usual, I arrived in the morning for a visit; we were both to set off with guns to a neighboring ravine frequented by wild boars. I found Joszt in a serious, collected mood. He said little, as if taken up with a stubborn thought; he shot badly, absentmindedly. In the evening, upon our parting, he shook my hand warmly and gave me a sealed letter in an envelope without an address.

"Listen, Roman," he said in a voice shaky from emotion. "Important changes are going to occur in my life; it's even possible that I might be forced to leave for a long time, to change my residence. If this happens, open this letter and send it to the enclosed address; I won't be able to do this for various reasons that at present I cannot mention. You'll understand later."

"Are you going to leave me, Kazik?" I asked in a voice choked up with pain. "Why? Have you received some bad news? Why are you so unclear?"

"You've guessed it. Last night in my sleep I saw again that dilapidated house, and inside the figure of someone very close to me. That's all. Farewell, Roman!"

We fell into each other's arms for a long, long moment. In an hour I was already at my place and torn apart by a storm of conflicting emotions, I gave orders like an automaton.

That night I couldn't sleep a wink, and I paced the platform restlessly. At daybreak, unable to endure the uncertainty any longer, I phoned Szczytnisk. Joszt answered immediately and thanked me sincerely for my thoughtfulness. His voice was calm and assured, the content of his words cheerful, almost playful, and they had a soothing effect; I breathed freely.

Thursday and Friday followed quietly. Every couple of hours I spoke to Joszt by telephone, every time I received a reassuring answer: Nothing important had occurred. Likewise, Saturday was similar.

I started to regain my composure, and retiring for the night around nine in the staff area, I chastised him through the telephone about tawny owls, ravens, and similar portentous creatures, who, unable to find their own peace, disturb the peace of others. He received my reproaches humbly and wished me a good night. Somehow, I managed to fall asleep soon thereafter.

I slept a couple of hours. Suddenly, in the midst of deepest sleep, I heard a nervous ringing. Half awake, I tore myself away from the ottoman, shading my eyes from the blinding light of a gas-lamp. The bell called again; I ran up to the telephone, placing my ear to the receiver.

Joszt spoke in a broken voice:

"Forgive me . . . for interrupting your sleep. . . . I have to send out . . . freight train number 21 . . . early today. . . . I feel a little strange . . . I will be leaving in half an hour . . . give the appropriate sig . . . Ha! . . ."

The fine membrane, after giving off a couple of grating tones, suddenly stopped vibrating.

With a loudly beating heart, I listened intently, hoping to hear something more—but in vain. From the other side of the wire came the hollow silence of the night.

Then I myself started to speak. Leaning into the mouthpiece of the telephone, I threw out into space impatient words, words of torment. . . . A stony silence answered. Finally, staggering like a drunkard, I went to the back of the room.

I took out my watch and glanced at the dial; it was ten minutes past midnight. Instinctively, I checked the time with the wall clock above the desk. A peculiar thing! The clock had stopped. The immobile hands, one on top of the other, marked the twelfth hour; the station clock had stopped ten minutes ago—that is, at the moment of the sudden cessation of talking on the other end of the line. A cold shiver ran down my spine.

I stood helpless in the middle of the room, not knowing where to turn, where to begin. For a moment I wanted to get on a trolley and drive on as fast as possible to Szczytnisk. But I stopped myself. I couldn't desert the station now; my assistant wasn't present, the staff were asleep, and a freight train could drive up to the platform at any moment. The safety of Krepacz rested squarely on my shoulders. Nothing remained but to wait.

Therefore I waited, pouncing from one corner of the room to the other like a wounded animal; I waited tight-lipped, going out every minute to the platform to listen for signals. In vain, for nothing announced the coming of the train. Therefore, I returned to the office to circle the room again a couple of times before renewing my attempts with the telephone. Unsuccessfully. No one answered.

In the large station hall, glaringly lit with white gaslight, I suddenly felt terribly alone. Some type of strange, vague dread seized me with its rapacious claws and shook me so strongly that I started to tremble as if in a fever.

Weary, I sat down on the ottoman and buried my face in my palms. I feared looking ahead of me, lest I glimpse the black hands of the clock that indicated the unchanging hour of midnight; like a child I feared glancing around the room, so as not to see something terrible that would chill my blood. Thus, two hours went by.

Suddenly, I gave a start. The bells of the telegraph were ringing. I jumped to the table, eagerly setting in motion the receiving device.

A long white tape slowly groaned out from the ticker block. Leaning over a green rectangular woollen cloth, I clasped in my hand the creeping ribbon and searched for any marks. But the roll had no writing on it; no sign of an etching needle. I waited with strained eyes, following the ribbon's movement. Finally, the first words appeared in lengthy minute intervals, words mysterious as a puzzle, assembled with great difficulty and effort by a hand shaky and uncertain. . . .

". . . Chaos . . . gloom . . . the incoherence of a dream . . . far away . . . grey . . . dawn . . . oh! . . . how heavy I feel . . . to break away . . . abomination! abomination! . . . a grey mass . . . thick . . . puffy . . . finally . . . I've separated myself . . . I'm here."

After the last word came a longer pause of several minutes; the paper continued to spin out in a lazy billow. And again the marks appeared—now with a certain assuredness, more resolute:

". . . I'm here! I'm here! I'm here! My body is lying there. . . on the sofa . . . and it's cold, brr . . . it's slowly disintegrating . . . from within . . . Nothing matters to me anymore . . . Some waves are coming . . . large, bright waves . . . a whirlpool! . . . Can you feel this tremendous whirlpool? . . . No! you're not able to feel it . . . Everything before me is strange . . . everything now . . . A wonderful vortex! . . . It's grabbing me . . . with it! . . . It has me! . . . I'm going, going . . . Farewell . . . Rom . . ."

The dispatch suddenly broke off; the apparatus stood still. Then, apparently, I lost consciousness and fell to the floor. So, at least, claimed my assistant who turned up at three in the morning; upon entering the office, he found me lying on the ground, my hand wrapped in sashes of telegraph paper.

When I came to, I asked about the freight train. It hadn't arrived. Then, without hesitation, I got on the trolley, and in the midst of vanishing darkness, I started the motor for Szczytnisk. In half an hour I was there.

I noticed immediately that something unusual had occurred. The typically quiet and lonely station was filled with a throng of people crowding about the staff office.

Forcefully pushing aside the mob, I cleared a path to the inside. Here I saw several men leaning over a sofa on which was lying, with eyes closed, Joszt.

I thrust away someone and sprang to my friend, grabbing him by the hand. But Joszt's hand, cold and hard like marble, slipped out of mine and fell inertly beyond the edge of the couch. On a face fixed by cold death, in the midst of tousled, luxuriant grey hair, a serene, blissful smile was spread out. . . .

"Heart attack," explained a doctor standing next to me. "At midnight."

I felt a sharp, shooting pain at my left breast. Instinctively, I raised my eyes to the wall clock above the sofa. It also stood still at that tragic moment; it also indicated twelve.

I sat on the sofa by the deceased.

"Did he lose consciousness immediately?" I addressed the doctor.

"On the spot. Death occurred exactly at twelve, while he was transmitting a dispatch through the telephone. He was already dead by the time I arrived ten minutes later."

"Did someone telegraph me between two and three?" I asked, my eyes fixed on Joszt's face.

Those present glanced at one another in amazement.

"No," answered the assistant. "That's out of the question. I entered this room around one o'clock to take over the deceased's post, and from then on I didn't leave the premises even for a second. No, stationmaster, neither I nor any other member of the staff used the telegraph tonight."

"And yet," I said half-aloud, "this night between two and three I received a dispatch from Szczytnisk."

A hollow, stony silence ensued.

Some type of weak, indolent thought was evolving with difficulty into my consciousness.

"The letter!"

I reached into my pocket; I tore open the envelope. The letter was meant for me. This is what Joszt had written:

Ultima Thule, July 13th

Dear Roman, I am to die soon, suddenly. The person whom I saw tonight in my sleep at one of the ruin's windows was I. Maybe shortly I will fulfill my mission and choose you as an intermediary. You'll tell people the truth, you'll bear witness to it. Maybe they'll believe that there is another world. . . . If I succeed. Farewell! No! Be seeing you—one day on the other side. . . .

Kazimierz

Visit the Stefan Grabinski website:
www.stefangrabinski.org